# DRAGON'S SECRET

## RED PLANET DRAGONS OF TAJSS BOOK FOURTEEN

### MIRANDA MARTIN

# CONTENTS

## NORA

*a* group of Zmaj approaches and I deliberately turn the other way, not wanting to interact if I don't have to.

Their gruff manners are exhausting to deal with. Delilah's earlier advice not to take their attitudes to heart makes sense. After all, they're under a lot of stress and fully on edge, ready to spill blood at a moment's notice because of the threat of the invaders.

Walking on eggshells is a familiar feeling. I had to on the ship before we crash-landed here on Tajss, and again when I was in the tunnels with Annabel. At least this isn't anywhere as bad as that second one. Towards the end there, Annabel was kind of losing touch with reality. She let her position as our group leader go straight to her head. Do not pass go, do not collect two hundred. Then, like now, I fell into the auto-nurturing mode that's kind of second nature to me.

"Come on guys! Time for bed!" I call out to the dragonlings.

Zoe, Elneese, and Ganeese are under my care while their

parents are out on patrol. They're great kids, but like all children—dragonlings included—they do take some wrangling.

"Not yet, Nora!"

"Just a little bit longer!"

"What if we just played one more game?"

I chuckle, shaking my head. "I already gave you fifteen more minutes. Remember our deal? It's time for bed now."

"Can we have a bedtime story?" Zoe pleads, changing tactics as she looks up at me with her big eyes. "Please?"

"Please?" the twins chime in immediately afterwards.

I laugh, knowing they've got me wrapped around their chubby little fingers, but not really minding. How can I when they're just so squishable?

A mix of both their tough Zmaj fathers and their human mothers, all three of them are so adorable I just can't stand it. Their chubby little faces, their tiny horns and tiny wings, they're the cutest things that I've ever seen. Problem is, sometimes I think they know it and take full advantage of the fact.

"Okay," I say. I give in without much of a fight at all. "If you get into bed, I'll tell you a story."

It'll help them sleep anyway.

They all whoop with excitement, running over to their pallets, kicking off their shoes to jump in.

As I watch them slide under the covers and settle in, giggling and talking among themselves, I can't help but fantasize about perhaps one day becoming a mother to a child just like them.

Not that I have any real prospect at the moment. I feel a pang at that thought, like I always do these days. None of the gorgeous dragons even noticed me before they mated with the any of the other women.

It isn't like I can't see why.

I've always been the shy type, definitely not as bold as a

lot of the females who survived the crash. I don't draw a whole lot of attention, and I don't particularly want to either. It's no wonder nobody looked at me. I'm always trying to blend in, fade into the background.

I know that.

Maybe the thoughts are self-critical, but the facts are also just what they are.

And now, the depressing reality is there aren't any Zmaj left for me to mate with, even if they noticed me. All of them have been coupled up. As I sit down with the little munchkins and start telling them the story of *Aladdin*—one of my favorites on the ship—I think about that.

It's not that I'm envious of everyone who has found their mate. I'm actually really happy for all of them. It's really good to see so many pairs now, to see how genuinely happy they all are with each other. It gives me hope for the future, hope for our civilization here on this alien planet.

When our ship crash-landed here years ago now...wow, has it really been that long? The thought kind of boggles the mind.

I never expected to be where I am today, though I guess I didn't really know what to expect or even hope for after the ship was attacked, after our separate scouting vessel crashed some distance away from the main ship. Our small group was lucky enough to be saved from some of the dangerous beasts here on Tajss by a lone Zmaj, which I'm forever grateful for.

But the life we lived after that rescue wasn't great. My particular group of women spent so much time underground in those tunnels with Annabel—our leader from our time on the ship—I really didn't have a whole heck of a lot of optimism for the future. We were just trying to survive the oppressive heat, living under Gomul's protection, eating what he hunted and what we could gather down there.

But things are so different now.

Looking down at these babies, I have hope, a lot of it, a warmth in my chest that I didn't even realize I was missing until it reinstated itself there.

But...

But.

Lately, I've been battling the feeling that I am going to end my days here on Tajss alone. Playing the role of Mary Poppins. Not that I have anything against Mary Poppins. She was my favorite classic character on the ship, the fun children's movie never failing to bring a smile to my face even as I grew older. I guess I just never anticipated that I would fall into that kind of role in real life.

I always thought I would end up with someone, that I would have babies, have my own family. The dream was always hazy, nothing pinned down, the man's face blurry, the children simple stand-ins for real ones. I'd had that idea forever, and I never thought it wouldn't at least be a possibility for me.

When we crash-landed here, that dream got put on the back burner due to circumstances. We didn't have anyone around except for an older Zmaj. The men in our group were all killed during the initial guster attacks when we first landed here, having no idea of the level of danger we would be facing.

But when Kate finally rebelled against Annabel's tyranny, our lives changed. A bunch of us who were also sick of living under the petty tyrant's thumb jumped on board to leave those dark and miserable tunnels. And we soon found out that there were many more survivors from the ship. And a lot of them were already in relationships with various Zmaj males.

I remember my initial wonder at that, my joy at seeing

babies, seeing children once more. The possibility of having a family was once again a reality.

But now...

It seems like it isn't anymore. Like that dream is once again an impossibility for me. This isn't the way I saw my life going, not even little bit. But we're not on the ship anymore, Toto. Gotta roll with the punches. So I try real hard not to let it get me too down.

I'm alive, and though life isn't perfect, I need to make the best of it. What else can I do? Curl into a ball and wail in lamentation every day? So not my style.

"...and they live happily ever after," I finish, having gone through that same story so many times that I don't even have to stay focused on it to tell it coherently anymore.

"Again!" Zoe cries out as soon as I finish.

I laugh, shaking my head.

"I think that's enough for tonight." I lie down next to Zoe to keep her company. "Here—I'll wait until you're asleep."

Elneese and Ganeese already look like they're having trouble keeping their eyes open, their blinks growing longer each time as they struggle to keep them open. But Zoe is wide awake as usual. She snuggles in close and takes hold of my face in her small, soft hands. I let her turn it so I'm gazing directly into her eyes.

I'm about to make a joke, but something in those familiar eyes stops me. They're too serious, too knowing in that cherubic face, like she might be able to discern my thoughts, my fear that I am going to be a spinster, alone forever.

Which is ridiculous. How would she know what I'm thinking? She's just a child.

I frown, opening my mouth to ask her what's wrong, why she's giving me that look. But before I can, an image appears in my mind's eye.

A Zmaj male.

One I've never seen before. He's tall, over seven feet like all the other Zmaj I've seen. Handsome, with a chiseled face and golden eyes set under level brows. As if that isn't enough of an attraction, he's jacked. Really jacked. Wide shoulders and muscles that tell the story of a more-than-active life.

When his leathery wings flare out and he turns to the side, I see the flick of his strong tail, the sunlight glinting off the red-orange tint of his scales. The small horns on his head are somewhat obscured by the shoulder length dark hair, messily windblown. His tanned skin and scales gleam under the Tajss suns, his health and vitality clear in the image.

Gorgeous. That's the word that comes to mind. I only see him for a split second, but it's like every detail about him is burned into my memory immediately.

Then the image is just...gone.

Poof.

And I'm looking into Zoe's eyes again.

I swallow, taken aback, but doing my best not to let it show. I don't want to scare her. Even though I'm freaking out a little on the inside. I have no idea what that was, but then something pops into mind.

There's been gossip that Maeve and Padraig have been developing a weird telepathic connection, and that it's somehow linked to these adorable dragon babies. Maybe this is connected too? I don't know, it sounds crazy but...seeing this after hearing that... it holds more significance, doesn't it?

I keep my face as neutral as I can while I wait for Zoe's eyes to slowly close despite herself. I can't be sure, but it looks like maybe whatever that was took some energy out of her. When her little hand falls limply off my cheek, I settle it next to her as I carefully stand up from the pallet.

I take a moment to just watch her innocent, sleeping face. Doesn't look like the face of someone with woo-woo powers, but I guess that doesn't matter. Shaking my head, I make my way out of the room silently.

I go over the details of the image, the details of the Zmaj I saw as I walk out. I don't want to forget them. It could be important. And it isn't like it's a hardship.

I head over to the cooking area while I keep that image as firmly in my mind as I can. Penelope is already there. She always has something to write with.

"Penelope, do you have a notebook on you?"

Her bright green eyes light up at the question. "Yeah, sure! Hold on one second..." She pats her pockets and pulls out a small notebook from a back one, handing over crude writing utensils too.

"Thanks so much."

"Yeah, no worries!"

I open the book up to a blank page and sit down in the corner. I have to press on the charcoal a little hard to make anything appear on the paper, but I make it work.

Bringing the image back to mind, I sketch the Zmaj I saw, trying to get everything down on paper before I forget it. I can't help but think there must be some kind of significance to the image I was given.

And the feeling he gave me. I haven't felt like that upon seeing someone in...well, ever.

I'm so focused on getting every detail down that I don't realize anyone is approaching until Arawn walks in. I immediately cover the drawing. It looks damn suspicious, but I don't want him to see it, and I'm willing to look weird to accomplish that.

He raises a brow at me—hard to get much by that one—but he's conveniently distracted by his duties almost right away.

Bashir walks in directly after he does, taking his attention off me. Phew. Maybe it wasn't the greatest idea to sketch this out in a common area like this.

"Arawn, can I speak with you?"

"Yes, of course..."

Bashir leads him away to have a private conversation. Arawn gives me once last lingering look before they're out of sight, but that's it. I let out a sigh of relief. Thank goodness Arawn is so consumed by his duties.

I rip out the paper and fold it carefully with the drawing on the inside. I've learned the hard way that charcoal just rubs off if you're not careful. I slide my drawing to the very bottom of my pocket for safekeeping before returning the notebook to Penelope. She takes it with a smile, and I turn my focus to cleaning the area.

There's still food left untouched, so I gather it up and save it for those on patrols. They're bound to be hungry when they come back from their shifts.

Delilah walks in just as I'm finishing up, the former engineer looking as in control as ever. I always envy her that sense of self possession. Probably because I myself find it so elusive.

"Want to play some checkers?" she asks, leaning against the wall. "I don't really feel like going to bed yet."

"Sure," I agree. After getting that image—vision? —I'm definitely not anywhere near sleep yet either.

"Great. I need something to wind down."

I nod in agreement, walking out with her to one of the boards that are already set up in this common area.

The Zmaj took real hard to both checkers and chess, resulting in a bunch of sturdy versions of the games crafted and ready to use in a lot less time than I would have expected. They're always available for all of us to play now. Times like this, I really appreciate it.

As I settle in across from Delilah, I briefly consider telling her about the Zmaj I saw, but I don't know if I want to reveal that just yet. Maybe it's nothing and I'm making too big a deal out of it. Better just to sit on it for now. So I move on to small talk instead.

"Zoe is starting to fight bedtime more," I murmur, making a move on the board.

Delilah snorts.

"That's what kids do," she remarks. "Now if none of them made a peep when it was time to sleep, then I'd be worried..."

She goes off on the psychology of children, which I wouldn't have expected, since she was a former engineer on the ship. She's generally more of a by-the-numbers person, but I guess they aren't mutually exclusive. After talking about the dragonlings for a bit, we move on to the city gossip.

"Everything always leads right back to the invaders," Delilah admits. "But I did hear about the training with the kedis and some of the tomfoolery they've been up to. Apparently, they've run out onto the street with more than one pair of underwear."

"What?"

Delilah starts regaling me with stories of the cute felines embarrassing multiple people with their shenanigans, to the point where I'm doubled over with laughter, holding my stomach. God, I needed this. It's such a nice break from talk of the invaders. A slice of normalcy.

"Thank you for that," I say sincerely, wiping at my eyes. "I needed that."

She nods, making another move as her face turns serious.

"Yeah. I hear you. I'm at the point where I'm trying to grab at any slice of good I can while I can." She looks up at me, meeting my eyes. "Who knows how long we'll be able to have these moments."

I sober at that thought. She's right. With the threat looming over us at all times, and the possibility of the invaders actually succeeding in kidnapping people for those fighting rings they run...

Let's just say I'm all for grabbing at any normal moment I can. Realizing that all over again kind of takes the fun out of the game though. We keep playing for a bit longer, but then we decide to call it.

"Maybe we can resume tomorrow night," Delilah offers as we stand up to go back to our respective caves.

"Sure," I agree. "Goodnight."

She waves at me as she walks away.

I reach my little corner of the cave system and get ready for bed. I'm not sure if I'm going to be able to sleep at all as I slide into the thick pallet. There's so much to think about, so much to worry over. But I'm so tired, even my swirling thoughts can't keep me awake for long.

I drift off to sleep despite myself, but my brain doesn't just fade to black. Dreams start immediately, an odd conglomeration of the usual. The desert, the children, the people in my life. None of it makes much sense, just a jumbled tapestry of experiences, ideas, and emotions.

Until suddenly everything goes blank.

Even in my sleep I find the sudden shift strange. But I barely have a moment to acknowledge that before it changes again.

As if a television is turned on, a fresh image shows up on screen. I'm looking down from a distance, down at the familiar desert sand dunes on Tajss. There's a man traveling over them.

That I realize I'm hearing something, something that doesn't really match the visual. When I focus, I realize it's the familiar voices of the dragonlings. They're whispering in a chorus. I strain to hear what they're saying, constrained by the fact that I don't really have any ears here. But I manage to pick out the words. Not that they end up making much sense.

"The Enforcer is coming to free us all."

That Enforcer? Is that what they said?

I try to focus on the man below, trying to see more clearly, but that image cuts off abruptly before I can make out much more than the fact that he's a Zmaj.

My eyes snap open.

I'm back in my pallet once more. My heart is pounding, my sheets soaked with sweat.

What the hell was that?

I lie there, trying to analyze what I just saw, trying to piece together something more now that I'm fully awake, but I don't come away with any more than I already know.

It feels like a message. A really strange message.

As I play it over again, I have a feeling that there's more to that dream than meets the eye.

Damned if I know what it is.

## 2

### ARCHION

*T*he buffeting wind forces me to squint as I watch the point where the suns meet with the sand.

I adjust the scroll on my back, protected in a leather carrying case for the journey. I must return it to the Order. It is the goal that drives me across the desert. After taking a deep breath, I slide down the dune and continue on my journey.

There's still much of the desert to cross, so I push my body as quickly as I can go, continually scanning my surroundings, watching for any threats. Tajss is a dangerous place. Even more so now.

At the moment that thought arises, a stray sound has me slowing. I crouch to lower my center of gravity and place each step with the silent accuracy of a hunter. I climb the dune in front of me to gain a better vantage point. When I crest the mound, I see the source of the odd clicking sound immediately.

My jaw clenches. Invaders. A large camp of them. The new danger to be found here as of late.

Elongated heads covered with textured blue skin and

eyes of full black under heavy brow ridges, they look nothing like anything else here on Tajss. Their lipless mouths are bordered by a tusk on either side, so curved in front that they almost touch. Each of them has six arms in total, three on each side, with the middle being the largest and most functional. Those large central arms end in three fingered hands with one joint per digit, tipped with sharp black claws at the ends. The other four are thinner and clearly weaker, ending in pincers rather than hands. As always, everything but the head, hands, and feet are covered by a brown armor reminiscent of an insect carapace.

All of them carry the odd emblem of a stylized yellow pincer on a brown background, sewn onto the left side of their chests.

As I watch, one of them opens its mouth, displaying sharp teeth as it lets out a staccato sound. It is not nearly as loud as the roar that I know they can release during battle.

I scan them for a moment, considering my options. It is the middle of the day, which makes it more difficult to move past them without detection. It also would not hurt for me to gather more intelligence on the strange aliens. Considering both of those points, staying and watching seems the most logical thing to do.

I move carefully, burying my body in the sun-warmed sand so that I will be more difficult to see. Then I lie there and watch, only shifting my eyes as the busy camp moves in front of me. I take note of their communication with each other, the hierarchy that appears to exist. Once the suns set, I will sneak past them and continue on my way. But even though I make no progress on my journey, it behooves me to stay and learn. I watch for some time, the suns above slowly lowering in the sky as I do. It will not be much longer before I can extricate myself from the sand and move past this encampment. Unfortunately, the exit is not as simple as the plan.

I freeze when I hear the sound of footsteps drawing closer. They are not urgent or particularly purposeful, so I stay motionless in the sand hoping the invader will simply pass me. It is likely one of them on patrol, so all I can do is hope that its attention is focused outwards, away from the camp, rather than inwards. I hold my breath, not daring to move, even enough to draw in air.

But I cannot control where the invader steps. I feel it set its foot down on me, catching it on my leg. It stumbles above me with an alarmed cry. I do not wait to see what it will make of the stumble. This close up, now that it knows something is here, there is no chance that it will overlook me.

I jump to my feet in a burst of sand, spinning my lochaber around to hit the unsuspecting invader in the side.

He cries out, but by that point, I already hear the cries and footsteps of others approaching. They heard his first alarmed yell.

When the first stumbles to the side and falls to the sand, I turn to see the others. I know there are too many before I even see them, and that I am much too outnumbered to stay and fight.

Assessing that quickly, I rush towards the few invaders directly in front of me. If I wait too long, they will amass, and then I might not be able to fight through them. The three directly in front of me attack all at once, but I only sustain a few blows from their main arms before I cut one down and use my wings to leap over the group.

I do not bother attempting to incapacitate any of them. More will just take their places. Better to make my escape now.

As soon as I am over them, I run, extending my wings to lessen my weight and skim over the sand.

When I look back, the group is running after me. But they are not built for the terrain here. It is more difficult for them to cross the sand, sinking in with each step as they do.

However, they are still fast enough that I have to keep moving to avoid capture. I cannot allow them to take possession of the scroll. They can never get their hands on it. That knowledge beating at me, I push myself even harder.

I know I can outpace them, but I do not know for how long they will give chase. I must keep moving. I must avoid capture.

When I look back after a short period, I cannot see them anymore, but I dare not stop.

Despite my desire to sleep.

Full sleep is a luxury that beats at me, that I crave almost like a starving man. I have not been able to lie down and settle into a deep sleep for days. Instead, I have been subsisting on the half-sleeping meditative state that allows my body to rest while I can continue to run. It is not nearly as effective as actual asleep, perhaps half as rejuvenating. But the state is very helpful when traveling long distances.

The Order developed it specifically for cases when one must keep moving past exhaustion.

It is not a perfect solution as then I cannot fight or engage in any other activity that requires the full use of my mind. But for an instance such as this when I have pursuers and I cannot sleep, it is the best solution. So I sink back into that now-familiar meditative state, and continue to move forward, the world dimming around me as part of my mind shuts down to rest. However, the section of my brain meant to be aware of potential threats continues to scan the area around me. A necessary precaution.

When the suns start to dip even more and the light starts to dim, my senses are super heightened and aware of everything around me. I know how to deal with of the worst beasts in the area, but the invaders are, as of yet, a more unpredictable variable. That does not mean I am safe from the beasts, just that they are a surmountable threat.

I continue running, the thinking portion of my brain resting. I manage to cover a solid portion of the sand in good time.

Movement on my periphery has my brain re-activating, coming out of that meditative state.

I turn towards the large shadowy mass that catches my attention. The starlight highlights its silhouette, the glittery eyes. The sheer size of it, combined with the distinctive trunk and tusks, tell me exactly what it is as it barrels towards me.

Cherepakh.

As it nears, I can see the segmented shell covering its back, head, and the otherwise-vulnerable underbelly. The large ears are flapping as it runs, allowing it to hear even the tiniest sounds at long distances.

It has likely been tracking me for some time.

Gripping my lochaber, I come to a stop and turn towards it. I will not be able to outrun it.

It lets out a trumpeting sound with its trunk, the move-ment showing off the sharp teeth at the end of it, the starlight also gleaming off of the teeth lining the tusks themselves.

Its sheer size makes it dangerous enough, even without the added weaponry of its tusks and trunk, let alone the armor of its shell.

But it has its own vulnerabilities. The four eyes, one set above the other, and its limbs, covered in a thick hide, but softer than the shell. The trunk and mouth are also good targets.

I feel the ground trembling underneath me as it rushes towards me.

My hearts are pounding as I assess the best way to attack.

When it lowers its trunk, opening up the field for its eyes, I decide to aim for them, using the target it has decided to give me.

I wait until the right moment, despite my body's desire to move, to get out of the way of the massive creature. When I judge the time is right, I crouch and leap into the air, using my wings to gain lift and my tail to steady myself.

I do not swing the lochaber back as far as I would for a stabbing blow. Accuracy is what I need for this maneuver, not strength. At the apex of my leap, I slash across the top pair of eyes, almost delicately. When I turn the lochaber and slash back the other way to get the bottom pair of eyes, I succeed in fully blinding the creature.

But I don't succeed in escaping completely unscathed. The trunk slashes at me, the sharp teeth scrape against my side as I continue the leap over the creature.

It is screaming from pain and confusion, its sight completely taken away.

But I do not make the mistake of believing it safe now. Wounded creatures are often the most dangerous, moving unpredictably. And it still has its hearing.

Ignoring the sting of the shallow cuts in my side, I deliberately move quickly. I do not want it to zero in on my position through sound. I know it will be more difficult for it do so if I move fast.

I watch its ears swivel as I move to the other side, slashing at the tendons at the back of its hind legs. I manage to incapacitate one leg, but not the other before it whips around, its trunk flying at me again. I slide under its body and over to the other side before it can make contact.

When I turn towards it again, the hind leg that I targeted successfully is dragging behind it rather than helping it move. With the cherepakh hobbled now, I can move back around to its head more easily. Distracted by pain, it does not realize that I have changed position.

When it opens its mouth to scream this time, I am ready with the lochaber pulled back, the blade aimed. I shove the sharp tip straight into the cavern of its mouth, angling it up to cut straight through to its brain. It takes some force for me to hear the crack of the skull under my blade. I grunt as I try to shove it in as far as I can with the large creature still struggling.

One moment it is attempting to pull away, and the next, it goes limp.

Dead.

I take a moment to catch my breath while I stand there, relaxing my arms. Then, bracing my feet against its leg, I pull back using my whole body, my weapon sliding free by increments. It takes almost as much effort as the initial puncture.

By the time the blade is out, the cherepakh is starting to fall over on its side. The ground shakes as it hits with its full weight. I look down at the carcass. If I was closer to the Order, I would attempt to gather as much meat as possible. But it is just me, and all I need is enough meat to last me a few days.

Too much will only weigh me down and delay my journey even more. I pull out my large hunting knife and sharpening stone. I keep my knives and weapons sharp, but I give the knife a few strokes while I think about the best place to harvest meat from this shelled animal.

In the interest of time and effort, I cut into the meat along its hind leg, a portion not protected by the shell. Also cognizant of my possible pursuers, I make sure to be efficient. The creature is still as warm as it was in life by the time I pack away the meat in my bag and am on my way once more.

But this time, I find my instincts pulling me towards

another direction altogether, one I was not planning on going in.

I frown at that inexplicable draw even as I continue to move towards it, trusting my instincts. I look inward, attempting to see why I am being told to travel in this direction now. The answer comes to me in a feeling more than in words.

A softness, a particular kind of energy. I frown harder as I continue to skim over the sands. Females?

Yes, that fits with this feeling. Why do I have this intuitive sense that there is the presence of females in this direction?

I do not know. It seems preposterous. I have not seen a female in... I do not even know how long now.

The Zmaj females have been dead and gone for years upon years. This feeling should not exist. It seems impossible.

But I am not one to ignore my intuition, especially not one so singular, so very unusual.

I have a clear sense of female energy. I am sure of it. My inner self never lies.

I feel a burst of excitement flow through me as I increase my pace.

A new and different target now comes first.

3

## NORA

$\mathcal{T}$he dream lingers in my mind the next day when I join one of the teams gathering meteorite glass, filling in for Maeve. I'm still no closer to figuring out what it means. All I know is that it must be important, and that the vision and the dream must be linked. It's too much of a coincidence otherwise.

I bend over, brushing off the sand from another chunk of meteorite glass and placing it into one of the bins we've brought out for the project.

The meteorite showers are still frightening in that they can destroy things and also seriously hurt anyone caught out in them, but the special pieces of glass they create when the flaming rocks hit the sand are really useful. Now that we know we can use them to power technology, I for one am glad when I realize a meteorite shower is coming. It has definitely saved our hides a couple of times when the invaders attacked, forcing the battle to cease as everyone scrambled for cover.

I move over to another section when I see the sunlight glinting off more of the glass. As I pick it up, I glance around at the others. I'm out here with a group of both Zmaj and women, but Penelope, Olivia, and Fallon are spread out farther away. Too close for me to speak with casually.

The only one next to me is Padraig. I watch out of the corner of my eye as he continues gathering meteorite glass efficiently. The task doesn't take a whole lot of thought, and I find myself a little bored in the silence.

Maybe some small talk is in order. Clearing my throat, I jump right in.

"So...it's pretty hot, huh?" I mentally smack myself. Could I have started with anything more inane than the weather? Yeah, it's hot. It's hot every freaking day here. We're on a desert planet with two suns!

Padraig looks over at me briefly before turning away again to gather another piece of meteorite glass.

"Yes."

Okay. I need a question that needs more than a one-word answer.

"What do you think we'll do if the meteorite showers stop?"

It's a question that comes up now and then because we're starting to become so reliant on the glass for technology, including the shields that we use. Without the shielding around the Tribe's cave system for example, I don't think we would have survived the attacks so far.

"No use worrying." This time, he turns away and deliberately walks a few more paces to create some distance. Making conversation more difficult.

My shoulders drop as I take the clear message. As if his curt responses weren't hint enough. Still, I try not to take it personally, knowing it's because he's focused on his task. It isn't like he's a chatterbox around anybody else at the moment either. I sigh, moving on with my own collection.

Even though I can rationalize away the interaction logically, it still makes me feel even more like the odd man out. Displaced and unwanted. I try to shake the feeling, but it's one I've been having frequently enough that it's difficult to let go of. The anxiety that comes with moving farther away from the Tribe's base isn't helping either, I'm sure. Even as I think that, I hear Fallon pipe up.

"All right, I think we've basically mined everything in this section—let's move a little further out!"

I gather one of the lighter bins and trudge forward through the sand, my feet sinking in with every step. The desert really is the worst.

The Zmaj are so well adapted for it, their wings lessening their weight enough that they can actually glide across the sand rather than sinking in like the rest of us do. This is despite the fact that they weigh so much more than any of us.

I set the bin down and immediately look back towards the wall that was built to help protect the cave system. I can usually see it even from some distance away. The meteorite glass set in it sparkles in the sunlight to tell me where home is.

But we've traveled too far now.

I can't see it.

My stomach drops, even though it makes sense. We've been moving out steadily for some time now. But the lack of visual still hits me kind of hard. I have to steel myself to keep my fear at bay.

I take a deep breath, trying to push it away, to focus only on collecting the glass in front of me. No matter how much I tell myself that everything is fine, that I'm in a group, that we aren't that far from the Tribe in actuality, the sinking feeling in my gut remains. I just can't shake it, even as I force myself to continue with the mindless work. I feel on edge, my skin prickling with awareness, my heart beating too fast for the low level of activity that I'm doing.

This doesn't feel like the normal level of anxiety I get this far out from home base. It's almost like...I'm being sent it? Though that's not quite right either.

I shake my head, trying to tease out what could be happening. The feeling is growing even stronger now. And it feels like...like it's telling me...

Danger.

That there's danger nearby.

That danger is coming.

I don't know why I'm having this feeling, or even if I should put any stock into it. Am I having an anxiety attack? Is this what they feel like? Maybe this is nothing, just my own emotions run wild.

I take a few deep breath and try to get my mind off of it. Try to distract myself by taking in our new position, watching everyone else, even counting how many pieces of glass I've gathered. But it doesn't go away.

Not for hours.

Just grows inside me, almost a separate entity. I'm so on the knife's edge that I have to grit my teeth just to stay there and continue to act like nothing is wrong.

"*Duck!*" My head jerks up at Zoe's little-girl voice calling out to me, the tone urgent. She shouldn't be here, not this far out from safety! I glance around quickly, trying to spot her, but she's nowhere to be found. More importantly, nobody else seems to be alarmed. They're continuing to search the sand around us for meteorite glass. I go still as I watch them and realize the voice wasn't physical. I felt it more than I heard it with my ears.

I go through that thought process within a split second before I decide to just listen to the damn voice. Things have been too weird lately for me not to give some credence to it. And what if something terrible happens if I ignore it?

I reach out for Padraig who is only a couple of steps to the side.

"Get down!" I order.

When I grip his arm tightly, gesturing with my other hand, he looks over, his gaze alert. He isn't trying to ignore me now. He simply crouches without argument.

"You guys! Duck! Get down!" I yell urgently as I follow my own instructions.

"What?"

"Why?"

"What's going on?"

But even though everyone's asking questions, they comply with my order too, trusting that I know something they don't.

We're down just in time to avoid being hit by the first bolts from the invaders' stunning weapons, the crackle of sound raising the hair on the back of my neck.

If we'd all been standing, we would have been laid out on the ground right now. Defenseless.

I shiver at that realization.

Padraig looks up at the bolts from the alien attacker's weapons and then back down at me, his eyes wide.

"How did you—"

Before he can finish the question, he's cut off by the onslaught of more fire from over the dune.

"Create a barrier!" Padraig shouts above the din.

The Zmaj instantly jump into action.

Padraig, Ragnar, and Arawn immediately start moving, staying low to avoid being hit by enemy fire as they form a shielding line around the women with their bodies. I stay in the center with the other women as the Zmaj scan the area to locate the threat.

It is not as simple as tracking the origin of fire—it seems to come from multiple directions all at once.

While all of us are scanning the dunes around our position, trying to discern where they actually are, I see movement to the right.

The distinctive silhouette of a Zmaj warrior appears at the top of another dune. It's unexpected enough to be eye-catching since our group is all together.

But then I look closer...

My breath catches.

I recognize him.

And not because he's one of the Tribe, or because I've met him before. No. I recognize the handsome face, the orange red scales, from the vision Zoe gave me. He's the same Zmaj who's drawing still burns a hole in my pocket.

I can't help but stare. He's the most gorgeous person I've ever seen. I thought maybe I believed he was so stunning before because he was a dream, because he wasn't real. But now that I'm faced with the reality of him.... Even in the middle of the danger, my heart skips a beat.

His golden eyes scan the area, our tightly gathered group. If he's surprised at the sight of us, he doesn't show it, maybe because he's too busy with other concerns.

"Prepare!" he yells at us. "They are coming!"

After the quick warning, he turns his back to us, spinning his lochaber in a deadly arc as the first line of invaders rushes up.

He tears into the group, the Zmaj around us leaping forward to join with battle cries, their wings flaring, their tails whipping out behind them, the sunlight glinting off their lochabers as they swing the sharp-bladed staffs.

"Back to back!" Penelope yells.

Me and the other women immediately follow the order, forming a circle with our backs to each other, holding out our shock sticks for protection. The long, club-like sticks have metal prongs at the ends. With meteorite glass inserted into each one to power it, they can create a shock that will stun a creature about the size of a human, but also cause a good amount of pain for anything larger.

None of us are anywhere near as good at hand-to-hand combat as the Zmaj, but with the shock sticks helping, we can at least try to protect ourselves. That is definitely a step up from where we were before, when we had no weapons at all.

But the invaders never make it to us, even though we stand at the ready.

The Zmaj move powerfully, lopping off heads with their lochaber blades, using the blunt ends to pummel and to keep some distance when they need to, shoving attackers back. They move fast, using their wings to leap into the air and travel over a crowd, and to gain leverage when they need to.

All of them are an impressive sight. But even with all of them fighting, I can't take my eyes off of the mysterious Zmaj for long.

The wind blows my hair every which way over my face, and I struggle to hold it back with my hand along with the others beside me, squinting to avoid the sand getting into my already-burning eyes.

Through it all, my eyes remain trained on the new Zmaj. All of the Zmaj warriors are good, but he's better. I can see that even with my untrained eye.

He moves smoothly, his muscles strong and lean, the purposeful, powerful way he fights reminding me of the elegant wildcats I used to fawn over in the ship documentaries. Powerful, elegant, and above all, dangerous.

I've never had this kind of reaction to anyone. Not to any of the human men on the ship. Not to any of the Zmaj here on Tajss. I watch the muscle ripple across his back as he deals a particularly deadly blow, his clenching thigh muscles straining for purchase along the sand.

I swallow, feeling a rush of heat. Maybe I even swoon a little on the inside. Not that I'd ever admit it, of course.

Who the hell *is* that?

## 4

## ARCHION

*I* look down at the scattered corpses of the invaders. The odd brown armor they wear is not enough to protect them from the combined forces of this many Zmaj warriors, even ones not as well trained as those of the Order.

I can feel the thinly tethered bijass of the other Zmaj as I kick over one of the corpses and crouch down to inspect it more closely.

I have sworn secrecy to the Order. I can handle the distrust of these dragons. They owe me their lives in any case. They know that. Without me, there was more than a fair chance the invaders may have won.

As I rifle through the hidden pockets of the invaders' uniforms, I sense the others doing the same with the other bodies. I do not find anything worthwhile, coming away only with items of little use. Not all of which I recognize. But I have seen enough from that quick search. There is nothing here that will be helpful or useful to us.

I stand once more, looking over the Zmaj beside me before my eye travels over to the grouping of females. My instincts did not lie, though they did not tell me the whole story.

They are not Zmaj, clearly as alien as these invaders I am more familiar with. Their coloring varies, as does their height and overall size, but it is still clear they are all of the same race. My eyes drift back to a delicate-looking one with hair of a shiny brown, cut to frame her soft face. She is...arresting. I want to keep looking at her, but I force myself to look away lest I ignite more aggression from the others.

"We should push on," I announce. "If there are others in the area it is best to keep moving."

The Zmaj male with the particularly large arms bristles, taking a step towards me.

"You do not give us orders," he snarls in a low voice, obviously not taking kindly to my suggestion. "I am in command here."

I turn to face him, seeing his threatening stance. I do not want to escalate this.

"I do not mean to take your command," I respond in a neutral voice. "But I do not take well to threats."

His large fists clench at his sides.

I adjust my stance, ready for an attack. It would be unfortunate after offering my aid, but I will finish any fight they begin.

The female that my eye was drawn to her earlier takes a step towards us.

"You guys, stop! We're all friends here." Her voice is just as lovely as the rest of her.

But neither of us backs down at her attempt at an intervention.

Another Zmaj growls at me, his brilliant blue eyes narrowed. "Watch yourself," he warns.

"If you think I have let my guard down, you are quite mistaken," I say in a low voice.

My hands grip my lochaber a little tighter as I try to keep my eye on both of them. I will not be taken unawares. If they think me easy prey, they will find themselves sorely mistaken.

But before the tension comes to actual blows, another one of their group shifts to stand between us. A Zmaj. I meet his eyes, his red and orange scales a brighter version of my own.

"I think you should return with us to share what you know with the Elders of our Tribe," he says with a much more measured tone than the rest have been using.

I do not let my guard down though I do nod slightly. I would rather not fight, but I have no intention of revealing information to their Elders or anyone else. Still, I need to learn more of this group, so I do not refuse.

"I would be honored," I say, inclining my had respectfully. "It has been several weeks since I have enjoyed a hot meal." That much is true.

"Good. We can provide that much for you, especially after your help." He looks over at the first Zmaj, the one who seemed fully ready to fight. Their eyes meet, something passing between them.

With a curt nod, he steps back. "We should return home," he agrees roughly, turning away.

And so it is decided. Not that this means I have been accepted into their group.

The travel back to their home is not a comfortable one. I know everyone is looking upon me with suspicion.

I listen closely as we travel, attempting to absorb as much information as I can from the conversations they have among themselves. I learn the one in charge is named Padraig, that the aggressive one with the blue eyes is named Ragnar, and that the one who finally intervened to calm matters is Arawn.

I also learn that the woman who I cannot keep my focus off of is named Nora.

Nora.

A name as lovely as she is. Her silky brown hair, her soft skin, her feminine curves... All of it make my fingers itch. I want to touch her, experience that softness for myself. Even her voice is soft and somewhat quiet as she speaks with the other females near her.

She is alluring in a way I have no name for. Special. An unsuspecting treasure.

One who has no idea how perfect she actually is.

# 5

## NORA

*I* look over at the stranger again.

His name is Archion, though that doesn't tell us all that much. Not that it matters. Not to me anyway. I can't even hide how interested I am, my eye going over to him time after time while we travel back towards the Tribe's cave system. I'm consumed with curiosity and attraction.

He is just so, so...male, in the best way possible. He just oozes masculinity, from the hard muscle that covers his body, to his strong jaw and high cheekbones. Chiseled. That's the word that comes to mind every time I look over at him. And his scales are so pretty, a tinted orange or red that's both subtle and colorful.

I just can't stop staring. I trace his profile, the sun lovingly highlighting the planes and angles of his countenance, showing off his beautiful skin. It's an even, gleaming brown that my fingertips itch to touch.

When he looks over, his golden eyes meeting mine, I feel a bolt of heat go through me.

I force myself to look away, knowing I'm being obvious about my interest but unable to be any other way. I feel the same warm, glittery sensation every time he turns to look at me. Like I want to clench my hands together in front of my chest like a fawning anime schoolgirl. I feel the weight of his gaze still on me, lingering.

Is he interested in me too?

Am I just imagining it?

I don't want to get ahead of myself.

What are the odds that I run into an available Zmaj and that he's also interested in me? Probably not great. I don't want to set myself up for failure. Not that I seem to be able to help myself.

But... Isn't this an odd coincidence? I've been ruminating over the possibility of eventual spinsterhood and bam—Tajss drops a possibly available dragon at the group's feet. Dressed as a hero no less—and a hero he is.

Both because he jumped in to save us and because of his skill. He seemed to know the moves the invaders would make before they ever made them in the battle. He was always in the right place to counter, to attack where the invaders were weak.

I'm pretty sure that's why Arawn intervened before anyone's bijass could get really out of control. Maybe he was worried how well Padraig would actually hold up in a fight with him. Or maybe he just didn't want to antagonize someone with that much skill if we could use it instead. Maybe he was simply suspicious. I don't know. But I'm so glad the fight didn't happen.

It was touch and go there for a minute. I wouldn't normally get involved in something like that, not when I can't stand up to any of the Zmaj in a physical confrontation. But something about the stranger had made me step up, pushed me past my normal reservations. Not that it helped, but I'm glad that I tried.

At this point though, what lies ahead still remains to be

seen. Yes, there wasn't an outright fight. However, I'm still not sure how the Elders are going to react to the dragon, veiled in mystery as he is. And as he seems to want to be. He hasn't said much at all while we've been traveling so far. I somehow doubt he's going to suddenly spill the beans once we're home.

Penelope nudges me with her elbow.

I look over at her questioningly.

"You should talk to him," she whispers, jerking her head towards Archion. "Staring isn't enough."

"I can't do that," I whisper back, blushing. I don't even bother pretending I'm not interested. It wouldn't be true and I know how terrible a poker face I have.

"Do it—you totally should. What's the worst that can happen?" Fallon chimes in, coming up beside us.

"They're right," Olivia adds, leaning in. "You should talk to him. How else are you going to find out if you like him or not?"

I shake my head. They can pressure me all they want, but I'm not a pushover. Maybe I'm quiet, and maybe I'm not the most outgoing, but if I don't want to do something, I'm not going to do it. Yes, I've had slim...well, no pickings. But that doesn't mean I'm desperate.

Yes, I feel an attraction towards him, but I'm not fool enough to forget that the woman is always the prize, and the man the hunter. Especially with the Zmaj. If he's mine, he'll let me know. He'll come after me.

That doesn't mean that the wait doesn't make me a little antsy though. I glance over at Archion again. Waiting is actually...delightfully maddening.

The potential of the situation is enough to have me dreaming of a possible future with a partner like others have, with children. But I find myself carried away with the fantasy, even after I remind myself not to get carried away.

We haven't even really had a conversation yet. It's not time to start picking out our children's names. I mentally shake my head at myself. Slow your roll woman. If I—

"Stay back!" Archion yells from off to the side where he's been walking.

My heart clenches as I stumble to a halt with the other women. What's going on now?

"Shit, what is it?" Fallon mutters, echoing my thought.

But we find out before we can actually voice the question to him.

The sand bursts open nearby, releasing a nasty-looking giant earthworm-like creature with scales. But instead of a closed end at the tip, it opens a massive mouth full of sharp, shark-like teeth arranged in concentric circles going down its gullet.

I stare at it, mouth agape, stomach rolling with fear. Shit. It's a zemlja.

Archion doesn't wait for it to do much more than come out of the ground before he's leaping up into the air and slashing at it with his lochaber.

The thing hisses, spitting at him but missing.

I take another step back with the other women as we watch the saliva sizzle on the sand. Acid spit. How wonderful.

Heart beating even faster, I look back up to see that Arawn has joined in the fight, working in tandem with Archion to stab and slash at the creature. Once again, I'm struck by Archion's prowess in battle, the smooth way he moves, like he knows exactly where that thing is going to go before even it does.

The other Zmaj join the fight and make quick work of the creature without sustaining any injuries. Though I think Archion could have likely done so even just on his own. He's that good.

In the end, Ragnar distracts it by running tauntingly close. Archion leaps up, swinging the lochaber in such a hard blow that it half chops off the thing's head, leaving it attached but dangling. Eewww.

The long body jerks, the flesh colored skin glistening in the light as it slowly falls over onto the sand.

Dead.

"I don't think I've ever seen anything so disgusting," Fallon mutters.

I murmur my agreement, staring at the now-lifeless creature.

"Good fight," Padraig offers with a grin as the Zmaj warriors gather around.

Archion nods.

"My thanks for your help," he says.

I see the other Zmaj warming to Archion now, trust beginning to form. There's no denying he put himself on the line to protect the rest of us.

"We will take a break," Padraig announces after a few moments. "There are ruins nearby that we can reach quickly. After we rest, drink, and eat, we will continue."

Sounds good to me. I didn't even do anything and that fight feels like it's taken it out of me.

I wipe at the sweat on my brow as we turn towards the nearby buildings, dilapidated and obviously ancient. Clearly they're from before the Devastation, the war that set the Zmaj civilization back so many years.

I take a few deep breaths. The harsh Tajss suns always drain me faster than I expected them to.

At least the epis has made us better adapted to the desert climate here. I remember how terrible I felt in those tunnels before we left and found out there was a plant that could actually help us do so much better here on Tajss.

Though that doesn't mean that I'm not still grateful to be

out of the sunlight when we enter the shade of a ruined building. The roof is intact, and that's what I care about. I shrug my pack off my back and settle down onto the sand next to the other women.

The first thing I do is take out my water to take a drink, but then I realize I only have one sip left. Sighing, I lower the water skin from my face. Before I can ask anyone if they have extra water, a large hand appears in front of me, holding its own water skin.

My heart skips a beat. I know who it is right away.

I look up slowly, my eyes meeting Archion's. I feel that same sizzle of attraction flow through me as I look into his golden gaze.

I reach out to take the water from him. If my hand trembles slightly, only I know. I take a few conservative sips before I hand it back to him.

"Thank you," I murmur.

He simply nods at me, something passing between us as our eyes stay locked for an extended moment. Something almost tangible. I feel a warmth, as if his spirit is enveloping me, scanning me somehow. But that's crazy...isn't it? I don't even know anymore. After a few beats, he finally breaks the eye contact and steps away, releasing me.

I let out a shaky breath, looking away. I don't know what that was.

But he's holding himself at bay.

So I will, too.

## 6

### ARCHION

*W*e leave the ruins and continue to travel to what they say is their Tribe's home.

I glance over at the lovely Nora again, a movement that has become as regular as breathing. My eye is drawn to her again and again. Even when I am not looking at her, I am fully aware of her, of her voice, her footsteps, where she is in position to me.

I look away once more and deliberately push forward so I am in the lead. I cannot spend all of my time staring at an unknown female. So I do a circuit around the group, scouting ahead to ensure there are not more invaders nearby, or any other threats. I must keep the group safe. There are females depending upon me.

I move back when I do not see anything of concern, traveling with the group for a period before I push forward again. I scan the horizon, keeping my gaze deliberately unfocused as I take in the familiar desert surroundings. It is the best way to track movement. Not seeing anything this time either, I turn to go back towards the group.

Then a flicker of movement catches my eye. I turn back

in that direction and focus, scanning with more deliberation. I do not see anything at first, but then something moves from around a large rock. Something with a deep green, almost black hide. I know what it is just from that first glimpse.

And it is coming at us fast.

I grip my lochaber with both hands and ready myself as I yell back a warning to the others.

"Sorpola!"

I hear the flurry of movement behind me that tells me they heard me, but I keep my eye on the approaching creature.

Unlike most of the beasts with four limbs here on Tajss, it walks on its hind legs. The thick, scaled hide covers its massive body, punctuated with blade-sharp spikes on the tail. Its forelegs are short and curled up by its chest, basically useless. Not that it needs its arms when it has a wide mouth full of rows of sharp teeth in addition to that dangerous tail. The sight of it alone is intimidating.

I brace myself as it runs towards us, saliva dripping from its now open mouth, its three thick claws at the front of its feet digging deeply into the sand.

As it nears, it opens its mouth and hisses at me, displaying the deep-red interior. Not where I want to end up. So I'd better stay sharp.

When it is near enough that I can see its small beady eyes, I leap quickly to onto a dune at my left and bounce from there onto the sorpola's back. The hissing sound grows louder as I cut a deep gash from the base of its head to the middle of its back. It whips around to bite me, its breath hot and fetid with its previous kills as it wafts over me. But I am able to launch myself off of its back and away before it can get its teeth into me.

Then the other Zmaj rush forward, attacking at the same time. I adjust my own forays into the fight, looking for spaces in which I can be helpful. When I see it almost catch Arawn, I deliberately whack its foreleg to get its attention, distracting it from its prey. I quickly leap backwards, just barely avoiding its mouth again.

Padraig leaps up onto its back and digs his lochaber deep into the gash I have already made, slicing further into it.

It lets out a hissing roar, its tail whipping out, Ragnar moving out of the way of the deadly appendage just in time. Arawn uses the distraction to leap forward and sink his lochaber into the creature's vulnerable underbelly. I use the opportunity to leap across its front and slash just under its head as it throws it back.

When I land back on the sand in a crouch, I know the creature is near death before I even look. It has sustained too much damage. When I turn, I see the blood pouring out of multiple wounds as it tries once more to snap its jaws over Arawn, moving much more slowly. Too slow to be at all effective.

It shakes its head once, twice. Then death finally claims it despite its efforts.

I hear the females move closer in that silent moment after the death, as I and the rest of the Zmaj catch our breath, still ready for any threat that may present itself.

I also realize this is another kind of opportunity, at least for me. I step towards Padraig, extending my hand in friendship. I know I must make the effort as I am the outsider here, the one that is suspect.

He looks down at my offered hand. He does not respond at once. He just looks for long enough that I start to worry he will not accept the gesture. But then he meets my eyes again and reaches out to clasp my forearm in his strong hand.

"Good fight," he says loudly and clearly, ensuring everyone hears.

"Good battle," I agree much more quietly, smiling slightly in response. I can feel my shoulders relax.

Then it is as though an unseen barrier has broken. The others gather around offering similar sentiments, reiterating specific sections of the actual fight. I know helping to protect the group wins me a certain level of trust, but I also see that offering my own hand in friendship first ingratiated me further. Good.

"Come," Padraig finally says, halting the talk. "We must harvest the meat for the rest of the Tribe."

I am glad the beast will be used rather than left to rot. Padraig and the others seem much more accepting of me as all of us gather around the felled beast and begin to harvest the meat with our hunting knives.

As I cut into the thick hide, slicing into the meat, my gaze can't help but go to Nora now that the danger is over, as it has ever since I crossed her path.

She is the perfect sanctuary of a female. So easy to rest my eyes upon, to listen to.

I watch her secretly while I make quick work of the animal in front of us. It seems no matter what I am doing, part of my mind rests on her at all times. Even during the battle, I was aware of her location though I did not divert my attention to her. I do not think that will change. I realize that as we pack up the meat, every member of the group carrying what they are able to.

Then we continue on our way once more. As we do, my mind sinks into itself again.

The Order consists of only the highest skilled dragons in the land, only the best of the Zmaj. For generations, we have learned to keep ourselves hidden, dispersed in undisclosed groups across Tajss. Each group carrying a piece of the puzzle that we have been charged to protect by the planetary consciousness herself. Each piece deliberately veiled in mystery.

Now I have a new puzzle, a new mystery.

Nora. A mystery my senses secretly delight in.

This...human species is unfamiliar to my kind. But the females have certainly long been prophesied. Not in any kind of detail, but enough that we always knew the Order, the Zmaj, would go on somehow. There is no doubt in my mind that these human females are clearly the ones that were foretold. However, knowing females were to come and being in the presence of one so alluring...

I could not have predicted how I am reacting. It is not at all how I would have expected, had I thought about it. But it is not something I can control.

As we travel for some more time, I continue to sneak glances at her, my weakness glaring to me. In a fairly short time, we reach more ruins, these somewhat larger than our last resting stop. Tajss is riddled with these reminders of the past. There is a sadness to seeing what we have lost, but I also believe they are a testament to what we can achieve, and so are not associated only with negative emotions.

"We will take a short break here to eat, then we will travel the rest of the way without stopping. Tonight, we will be back home," Padraig announces.

Murmurs of relief ripple through the crowd as we trudge into another building that is falling apart. Time and the harsh conditions make themselves known on every structure if it is not actively maintained.

Meat is immediately taken out and set over a fire to cook, the delicious smells sending a hunger pang through my stomach. As I settle in next to the other Zmaj, listening to the murmur of conversation, I find myself enjoying the odd bonding taking place within the group. Perhaps they do not consider me one of their own, but I appreciate the inclusion nonetheless. Especially after so much time alone.

"Do you know anything of these invaders?" Arawn asks as we wait for the meat to cook. "It seemed as though you were familiar with them." It is a pointed question.

"I have seen them before," I admit. There is no reason to lie about that. "But I fear I do not know much more than you do about them. Have they attacked you before?"

Perhaps this is an opportunity to absorb information as well.

"Yes," Ragnar answers. "More than once..."

As we continue to discuss invaders, I decide against disclosing too much of what I suspect. About what my own Zmaj brothers know. These invaders are not random or here accidentally.

They are also a very real danger to us, a danger to be taken very seriously. The survival of every Zmaj and now every human on Tajss is at risk. However, information is power and knowledge should be doled out carefully. I need to know more about these people first.

To that end, I observe both the Zmaj and the human females while I sit and rest. Glances and touches as well as conversation are all enough for me to deduce that every one of the group is mated.

All save one.

Relief at that knowledge flows through me. It is possible her mate waits for her in the Tribe's home, but I do not believe that is the case. Not with the way she behaves.

I look across the fire at Nora, the warm light illuminating her soft features. She is a jewel so rare, so timid, I feel my protective instincts clamoring around her.

Just as I feel increasingly attached to this mission. Dangerously attached. In a way I cannot afford. I must control myself.

I look away from her lovely features, attempting to focus on the conversation with the other Zmaj about the invaders. I must not forget I am here to collect information.

Luckily, as Padraig said, we do not stay in the ruins for long before we pack once again and continue upon our journey. I soon realize our destination is actually not much farther. The first indication we are near is when sunlight glances off a wall. An obviously, deliberately placed wall, set in front of the cave system.

"Thank God we're almost there," I hear one of the females murmur behind me.

I understand the sentiment. The journey may not have taken much time, but it has been quite eventful so far. We have run into more than our fair share of danger.

When we pass across the wall, our arrival is hailed by a mixture of humans and Zmaj living in the cave system.

As I look around, I am struck by the curious blend of the two, shown everywhere I look. There are human females in what must be the kitchen area, cooking, using the pots and utensils that are obviously Zmaj made. Throughout the area that I can see, there are soft touches that most definitely did not come from the Zmaj, pretty things like fresh flowers in small vases, small pillows, little candles. I see two Zmaj stand up from either side of a square board that has smaller squares painted on it and small figures set on those squares in what appears to be a deliberate pattern. A game of some kind, perhaps? But not one of the many Zmaj games.

The cave system itself, of course, is obviously influenced by the Zmaj. From the way I can see things are ordered, to the wall built in a classic manner, all the way to the machine in the corner that appears to be powering the shields. I frown at the machine as I reconsider that. It looks to have used old Zmaj technology, but with changes. Perhaps another human touch?

I am distracted from that puzzle as I hear small, high-pitched voices that abruptly quiet down. When I turn back, it is to see hatchlings. I stare down at them, shocked.

Hatchlings.

It has been so long since I have seen a young one that I stare. I know it is rude, but I cannot stop. These adorable creatures are clearly a mixture of their Zmaj fathers and their human mothers.

Their soft, round faces are punctuated by tiny little horns, small translucent wings, and the suggestion of scales. But their coloring varies more than the Zmaj population's does, from their hair, to their skin tones, something they have clearly inherited from their human sides. We are a desert people after all, with dark hair and tan skin. While I stare at the small creatures, they stare back up at me with large eyes, as if just as shocked to see me as I am to see them. Why would that be? But I know they are shocked.

I heard them speaking just moments ago, but now they say nothing, simply staring at me with what appears to be awe in their eyes. As if I am a higher creature, something to idolize. I do not know what to make of it. Before I can gather words to say to these tiny people, Padraig speaks up once more.

"Everyone, this is Archion. We met him out in the desert while we were gathering meteorite glass. He helped us battle attacking invaders, as well as a surprise zemlja and sorpola." He looks over at me. "His aide was needed," he adds more quietly.

I hear murmurs among the gathering crowd before an older Zmaj steps forward. The conversation settles down around us. He is obviously a highly respected member of their Tribe.

"It seems as though you have had quite a journey back," he says, addressing Padraig before then turning his attention to me. "We would like to speak with you, Archion. But first—you must be hungry. We will eat dinner first."

The female in the kitchen area with the dark brown eyes takes that announcement as her cue.

"Food's up! Here, Archion," she addresses me directly, reaching out to take my arm. "Have a seat. We love all kinds of help here, and I'm really glad that you helped bring everybody back safely." She settles me down in a chair at a nearby table. "I'm Delilah, by the way," she adds almost as an afterthought.

"Thank you, Delilah," I say, taken with her genuine warmth.

"It's the least we can do," she replies, waving the gratitude off.

"I made a plate for you," a softer voice says from my left.

When I turn to look, there is the lovely Nora with a plate laden with food. Meat and what appears to be vegetables. They must have a garden nearby. I take the plate she shyly offers, feeling a rush of warmth.

"My thanks," I say, my voice lowering.

She nods and quickly backs away, her cheeks red with embarrassment. It only endears her to me further. I want to draw her into my arms, comfort her. But now is not the time. I do not know if it ever will be.

Before I sink into that thought, I am distracted by Arawn and Padraig settling down on either side of me with their own plates.

"How did you know the zemlja was coming?" Arawn asks before he takes a large bite of food. "There was no indication I could detect."

"Oh, well..."

I settle into a conversation with them, the words coming much more easily than I would have expected. I find myself actually enjoying the company, the food, the setting of this home. And it is a home. They have succeeded in making this more than just a cave. It will be difficult to part with the hospitality of the males, of Delilah.

Of Nora.

But I remind myself that I must. It would not be smart to become too attached here, when I know my stay will be necessarily brief. It is a sobering thought. Even so, before I'm aware much time has passed, my plate is empty and dinner is over. But I am not left to ponder what my next move will be.

Padraig stands at my side as soon as I am done eating, as if he was waiting for it.

"The Tribe Elders, Kalessin and Falkosh, wish to speak with you."

I look over to where he gestures towards two older Zmaj, one of which is the same Zmaj who spoke up earlier about dinner.

"Of course," I say, rising to my feet. There is no way not to meet with more of their leadership. So I follow them to a cave that is somewhat separated for privacy. I keep my face and body neutral, not wanting to show that I am worried or nervous in any way, lest they read too much into it.

"We appreciate the aid you have given to the Tribe," Kalessin begins.

"Yes," Falkosh agrees, watching me carefully. "We are truly grateful for that." I nod, knowing gratitude is not the reason for this meeting. I am proven correct quite quickly. "However, may we ask—where were you traveling to? What was your final destination? What journey did you delay in order to accompany our people safely home?"

The questions are measured, delivered carefully. They are clearly attempting not to cross too many boundaries, not to make me so uncomfortable that my guard will rise. Unfortunately for them, my guard never lowers. I know I cannot give too much away with my answers.

"Simply to my own home," I reply with just as much care as they have shown. I suppose it is true, as far as it goes. Their expressions do not change, the unreadable looks upon their faces showing just how wary they are of me. I do not blame them. They do not know of me, just as I do not know of them. But I still do not tense, attempting to appear as nonthreatening as I can. "But I wanted to ensure your people arrived safely, especially considering that the group included females."

That is true. I would have helped the Zmaj, but the fact that their group included females kept me from leaving after that initial invader attack.

I watch the Elders share a heavy glance. Perhaps I should not have mentioned the females. But to not acknowledge their presence at all would have seemed suspicious as well.

"I see," Falkosh murmurs, turning his attention back towards me after their silent conversation. "We realize you must be exhausted, so we will simply thank you once again for your aid." I incline my head once more. The less words I utter the safer it will be. "And, to show our appreciation, we would like to offer you accommodations for as long as you need them."

Ah.

"That is very generous of you." And it is. "I will impose upon your generosity to rest before continuing on my journey."

I know that they have more than one reason to offer me shelter. They want to glean more information from me if they can. They have noticed that I am not revealing any more than necessary. If I were the leadership of a large group like this, I would want to increase my chances of learning more too. Especially if a threat was a possibility. But they will only be disappointed. I will not reveal anything I have no intention of revealing.

"Padraig, if you will please show our guest to a free cave?" Kalessin says, addressing the big Zmaj where he has been waiting silently at the opening of the cave.

"Yes, Father," he agrees. Ah. They are family. I feel a pang at that. So much has been lost. "Come, Archion."

I nod, saying goodnight to the Tribe Elders before I follow him out.

There are some people still in the main area, some of them sitting across from each other and playing what I now gather I was correct about. The square boards are indeed games.

Padraig leads me to a small cave, walking in and lighting a few small candles with his torch before gesturing me inside. I look around at the neat little guest quarters, complete with a thick pallet, a chair, and a small table.

"You may ask anyone you see if you need anything," Padraig offers.

"My thanks."

"Of course. I will see you in the morning."

"Goodnight."

He gives me one last searching look before nodding and turning to leave, dropping the curtain back into place at the mouth of the cave for privacy.

When I am alone, I take off my pack, and the rolled-up scroll. I tuck the cylinder holding that precious cargo into the pallet rather than laying it beside the bedding as I do with my pack. I cannot trust that nobody will try to search my things, so I will just make it more difficult to do so while I sleep.

I don't plan to rest right away in any case. I am tired, but I must do something else first. After lowering myself to the pallet, I cross my legs and rest my hands on my knees, palms up. I stretch my hands and relax them allowing them to curl, to close halfway.

I take a deep breath. I close my eyes. I focus on my breathing. A deep inhale, followed by a long exhale. I feel my heartbeat start to slow, my energy start to spread. My consciousness expands, beyond the tight aura that is usually around me.

And there is that familiar maternal energy at the thin edge of myself.

Tajss.

I sigh as the warmth and welcome of the planet itself encompasses me. I settle in to commune with the source of the Order's sacred information.

## 7

NORA

"Can I use the scraps?"

"Sure," Delilah agrees, handing over the tops of the roots she has already used for her dish. "Have at it."

I murmur my thanks, taking the fragrant, delicate greens. I continue to work on my own dish, incorporating them into it. As I move over to my own cutting board in the kitchen area, I can feel Archion's eyes on me, his intent gaze heating my skin, making it feel sensitive and feverish under his regard. My self-consciousness is hyper intense because of it, my shyness rising. I try to push thoughts of him aside and focus as much as I can. It isn't easy.

When I first began apprenticing with Delilah, I proved myself a quick learner. I found out quite early on that I had a knack for cooking, and I discovered I enjoyed doing it. And now, with Archion still here, I have even more of an incentive to show what I have learned so far.

I concentrate as I measure out a fistful of the root tops. I want the special dish to be perfect. At the root of it—no pun intended—it's a simple stew. But I've been playing around with it, using what seasonings we have, and I think I've come up with a beautiful blend.

I sink into cooking, into chopping, tasting, seasoning. I feel at home in this space, in doing the simple but important task.

I make one last adjustment, dip another clean spoon into the bubbling mixture, and bring it up to my mouth to have a taste. I close my eyes briefly, focusing on the complex flavor. It's perfect!

"Time to put the food out," Delilah calls to me.

I nod, untucking the small cloth I keep at my waist while I'm cooking. As I plate the dish and set it out with the other food, I feel nerves rising, my stomach full of butterflies despite my confidence only a few moments earlier. I really hope everyone likes it.

Should I have added more salt? No, it was fine. If I touch it now, I'll just throw something off.

I watch as the other women and the Zmaj fill their plates and sit down.

Delilah is the first to taste it. I watch her as she takes a bite, leaning forward in my own chair in anticipation. Her eyes widen as she chews. Good or bad? I can't tell, damn it! Her eyes find me as I wring my hands under the table.

"Nora—this is great!" she praises after she swallows. "So good!" She takes another bite with apparent enthusiasm.

I look around at the others for confirmation, trying not to seem as eager as I feel. Do they like it?

"It is quite delicious," Ragnar says.

"Oh man, it's so good," Penelope agrees, taking a bite of her own.

"Really?" I ask, acting casual as everyone murmurs their approval.

"I wouldn't lie to you," Delilah offers. She points her spoon at me. "Not about food. That is serious."

She's right. She doesn't dole out compliments indiscriminately, not in the kitchen.

I feel myself sit up straighter, glowing from the compliments. It sounds stupid, but ever since Archion and I have crossed paths, I feel like a suppressed part of me has begun to rise. The part of me that I always tucked inside myself, kept covered up as I deliberately tried to fade into the background. For some reason, I just don't feel that need to hide myself right now. In fact, I kind of like drawing some attention, maybe showing off a little, as evidenced by how much I'm enjoying everybody liking this dish.

Delilah liking the food is the sweet icing on the cake. She probably will never give me her secret sauce recipe, but she's taught me a lot. More importantly, she's helped give me a sense of purpose among the Tribe, both in the kitchen and out. Her opinion really matters to me.

"Yes. Delicious indeed."

I look over at the deep voice, knowing who it is from the timbre alone. Archion watches me intently as he takes another bite, the words he just said taking on a new meaning. The others continue to rave over the dish, but I can't tear my gaze away from his. Not when I feel like he's undressing me with it.

I have to force myself to look away, to focus my attention on my food. He's been watching me all day, his attention like a heated brand upon my skin. I've never felt so aware of how I move, of my breathing, of just how I hold myself. I feel every part of me in a way I never have.

It's a little uncomfortable, but the attention is far from unwelcome, though I don't make a show of catching on to it. I just enjoy it all through the meal. Is this how the other women felt when they met their mates? If so, no wonder I'm not with any of them. I never felt anything even close to this.

After dinner is over, I see that Archion is still watching

me. I decide to busy myself by going into the children's cave again and telling them another story. That's enough attention for one night.

"Can you tell us about the genie again?" Zoe asks, looking up at me with those big eyes.

"Yes!"

"Yes, the genie!"

I laugh as Elneese and Ganeese chime in.

"All right. Everyone settle down on. I'll tell you the genie story again."

I settle into the story, deliberately telling the longer version. I don't want to go out while the communal games are still going, needing a break from Archion's all-encompassing gaze. By the time I leave the sleeping children, everyone has already gone to bed. Perfect.

That doesn't mean I don't dream of that hot gaze upon me, or that he's not the first thing I think of when I wake up the next day. Still, I can't just think of him all day and night. I have things to do.

The first thing on the agenda is packing up and loading cargo into the rover for the trip to the city. Candles, herbal salves, and crushed healing stone tinctures Errol has made according to orders received, all have to be carefully loaded into the vehicle for the trip.

As I wrap another candle and set it into a box, I find myself thinking about my life with the Tribe as I do from time to time. I really like it here, even blending mostly into the background as I do. I mean, I still usually prefer it that way, not really enjoying attention despite how much I soaked in the praise about my cooking last night. That was different for me, though I don't regret it.

I'm just so happy I followed Kate to the Tribe rather than staying in the city with the other women who were in our group. The time in the city was okay, but the Tribe felt like home the moment I arrived to help with the dragonlings and the births to come.

I love children. Being a midwife and a nanny is very fulfilling. I enjoy doing crafts, cooking and taking care of the farm as well, but the children are where my heart is. At least in this new iteration of my life. And now, with Archion here with us...I can't stop thinking about children. Privately, I indulge in the secret thrill of possibility as I continue to work. Nobody has to know I'm getting so carried away with the fantasy.

As the day wears on, I start to notice something that puts a damper on that particular dream. An odd tension in the air. By the time dinner arrives, I know I'm not imagining it.

I felt the cloak of distrust coming from the Elders all day, but at the communal meal that night, I can really sense the uneasy tension emanating from them, despite the fact that they're there to join in the festivities.

I watch them as they continually glance over at Archion. His presence is clearly the source of the tension. I keep a straight face, but a knot starts to form in my gut. They're trying to hide it, but their joint attention is subtly but surely fixed upon the newest addition. I don't know why, and I'm not sure what to make of it.

I do know that I feel protective over Archion in a way that doesn't quite gel with how long I've actually known him. Or how well I know him, which is not at all really. All I do know is that I won't sit back and allow them to harm him despite all the logical reasons why I shouldn't get involved.

I can't overtake them by brute force, but I can get to the city. I know Rosalind would intervene in any matters of injustice. She's reliable like that. I have that in my back pocket, but I really hope it won't come to that. These people are my family now. I don't want to move against them if I don't have to.

I keep an eye on the situation as I pretend to remain care-free, my role as someone who stays in the background serving me for once. Nobody's really paying attention to me.

I've never felt intrigue like this in the Tribe before and it's throwing me off kilter in a way I wouldn't be able to hide with too much attention on me. I've always felt only comfortable here, like I'm at home.

But my gut is now ringing with warning. And no matter how uncomfortable or awkward, I don't plan on ignoring it.

I look up, my eye going to the Elders once more, lingering there before I glance over at Archion, only to find his eyes trained on me. I feel that familiar rush at the eye contact. He doesn't look away when I meet his eyes, watching me steadily.

He appears calm, not at all perturbed by his surroundings despite being a stranger in a strange place. Definitely calmer than I am, but I don't think it's ignorance.

Something about his eyes... I feel like he knows that he's the object of not-completely-positive attention. Like he knows about the intrigue going on behind the scenes.

I don't look away this time, keeping that eye contact despite feeling my face flush with heat. I feel so much when I look at him. As I maintain that contact, I feel the attraction deepening between us. Well, at least on my end.

He continues to be difficult to read, even as his presence, his attention, sends tingles down my spine. This time, he's the one who averts his gaze.

I finally look down, my heart thumping hard.

It takes more effort that I want to admit hiding my reaction to him through the rest of dinner.

## 8

## ARCHION

*W*hen I go to my temporary quarters, my mind is still on Nora. I could sense her intuition regarding the Elders, her concern. Her protectiveness. Maybe I recognize that in her because I feel the same way towards her. I want to guard her, never let any harm come to her. I know I would put my own life at risk to ensure her safety.

While my interest is endlessly seized by the beauty, I feel the uneasy stir of duty to the Order. All of these feelings are competing with the place my attention should be, where duty demands it stays. But I cannot seem to completely separate myself from these emotions despite that knowledge.

When I wake the next morning, I resolve to keep better control over myself as I aid in the collection of meteorites from a light shower the previous night. The meteorite showers are a more common occurrence now, one that I am glad the Tribe is taking advantage of.

As I walk back towards my cave after my shift, my mind on this new society they are building here, a sound catches my attention. A feminine humming.

My footsteps slow at the arresting sound. I know instantly who it is. I am so attuned to Nora at this point that I would know her voice anywhere. The sound calls me to the spring she bathes in, one I notice the females have been sharing on a rotating clock. They treasure their time there.

I stay hidden, peeking out only briefly to ensure that it is her. I immediately hide myself again, not wanting to intrude on her privacy. I close my eyes and stand there, listening. Her hum blooms into a song I am not familiar with, weaving an enchantment around my hearts. A sure threat to my mission. But once again, the knowledge does not push me away from her.

As I listen, I cannot help but imagine her bathing, the glittering drops of water on her skin shining in the sun, her hair sleeked down to her head, revealing the soft contours of her face. I only saw a brief glimpse, but my imagination is strong.

I have heard the females call the spring their "spa", a concept similar to the pools used by the Order. Judging by what I have heard of their conversations thus far, bathing and water was an apparent luxury on their ship. Learning that their ship crash-landed on Tajss was not a surprise to me.

They are most definitely a new addition to the planet, clearly not adapted for the climate or the harshness here. If the other Zmaj had not procured epis for them, I do not think they would have survived this long. I am glad that the females found the other Zmaj. I could not imagine a world now without Nora in it, even though I just learned of her. It does not make sense, but perhaps it is not meant to.

I listen for as much time as I can steal, but I cannot linger for too long at the arch by the spring. I sigh, enraptured by this jewel of a woman. However, much as it pains me, she cannot be my priority. Staying for a moment past when I know I should, I continue on to clean up before I meet with Arawn again.

Morning patrols under Arawn's leadership are a simple exercise. My own teachers were far less lenient than he, but I do not voice that opinion as I follow orders. I doubt it would be met well, even apart from revealing more than I desire to.

When I see two of the other Zmaj irritably snap at each other, I mentally shake my head.

"Stay back," one growls.

"Control yourself," the other responds, a muttered rebuke with a flash of anger that they quickly control.

The dragons of the Tribe are in decent physical shape, but they lack full control over their bijass. That's a vulnerability that invaders will exploit given the chance. My own teachers would never have allowed such a lack of discipline. Again, I maintain my silence on the matter.

I am clear on my role here. I am simply a guest, not a part of the Tribe. I am certain my criticism will not be appreciated. So I keep my it to myself, running through the patrol around the cave system with Ragnar, doing my part before we turn back.

When we arrive, the females are in the kitchen preparing the midday meal.

Including Nora.

As I find myself doing every time she is in the vicinity, I watch her closely, studying her. Just like I would prey, though a completely different sort of adrenaline guides my actions in this matter. I want to know everything about her, want to absorb every morsel of knowledge. She strikes me like no other.

Even while she is in full view, she does not draw attention, a skill in and of itself. Her tendency to hide herself away, to shroud herself in anonymity only draws more attention for me. It goads me to chase, intoxicates me like clear attention from her might not. It is almost as if she knows, though I know she has no true idea of my intentions. Intentions that harden when I am alone with my thoughts of her.

I know she is aware of my attention, because her eyes give her knowledge away. When she glances over at me from time to time, her cheeks flush at my direct gaze. She is so tempting. Even while we eat, food that is in part prepared by her hands—making it even more delicious—I watch her.

Padraig takes a seat next to me.

"How were your patrols this morning?" he asks, beginning a conversation while he starts to eat.

"Smooth. No problems," I answer him, even as my attention continues to stray to Nora.

The end of the meal is something of a repeat of the first meal I had with the Tribe. Padraig stands up and looks down at me.

"The Tribe Elders would like to meet with you again," he says.

I nod, expecting it. Their concern and attention is clear to see whenever I am around them. Frankly, I am surprised they did not pull me aside earlier.

"Of course," I agree.

I follow him into the same secluded cave again, Kalessin and Falkosh already waiting there for us. The inquiry is brief, but pointed.

"We have not asked you too many questions, not wanting you to feel uncomfortable here," Kalessin begins. "But we must also look after the Tribe, our people."

"I understand."

And I do. I would not trust a stranger who I know nothing about in the Order either.

"We are glad you do," Falkosh murmurs, sharing a glance with Kalessin. "Now. We would like to ask you what your business is. What actually brought you out to the desert near us."

Ah.

Perhaps they believe I was gathering intelligence on them and took my opportunity when the invaders attacked to infiltrate. That would have been a good way to gather information about them, but I did not even know they were here.

"My brothers and I came up with a plan to lure the invaders away from our camp. We did not want the threat to draw even closer than they already had."

It is not the whole story, not even a majority of it. But it is all that I am willing to give, and I know the Elders cannot read me any more deeply than I allow them to. I would never expose my brothers simply to protect myself. There is a finality to my statement, a clear indication in my tone that I will not say any more. Even if they ask.

I know they understand that tone because they only share a glance before continuing. They do not ask me any more questions. But I am not so ignorant as to believe that means they trust me now.

"I see," Kalessin says after a brief silence. "We also had another reason to meet with you."

"Oh?"

"Yes," Falkosh agrees. "We would like to offer you a temporary post here with the Tribe, until such time as you need to return home."

I am certain they are seizing the opportunity to spy on me while they can, offering me this post simply to keep me here longer. Of course they also desire my skills. I know they have noticed that I am very well trained. Better trained than they are here.

However, I do not begrudge them the desire to learn more. I too have reason to stay longer. I feel a glimmer of humor. Perhaps we can all tacitly agree to continue to spy on one another.

"That is very generous of you," I say, inclining my head. "I will gladly accept."

Even without the offering of an official post, I have already begun helping where I can, so it will not be much of a change from what I am already doing.

"Wonderful," Falkosh says, his tone reserved.

But all of us are reserved in that small cave. Much more is going on underneath the surface of the conversation.

"Padraig will inform you of your new post and your duties," Kalessin says, nodding at Padraig.

Clearly dismissed, I say my goodbyes and follow Padraig out. I settle into the patrol I am assigned quite easily. Work I can do. It also takes me away from the sharp gaze of the Elders, allowing me a moment to relax somewhat, which I appreciate. Unfortunately, that small reprieve does not last very long.

Later in the afternoon, Padraig pulls me aside to speak with me once more.

"Visidion, the Tribe Commander, would like to speak with you."

"Visidion?" I ask. "The Tribe Commander?" I look around. "Why have I not met him?"

"My brother lives in the city nearby, another enclave of our society. He spends much of his time there, with his mate."

"Ah." Interesting. I would like to see the city that they have inhabited. This is a good opportunity. "How will I travel to the city?" I ask politely.

I know they will not send me alone. They would fear I may leave completely, and I have the impression they do not want me to leave before they glean more information from me.

"Errol will drive you in the rover, the vehicle the humans brought with them," Padraig explains.

I nod. And I also see another opportunity, one I take despite knowing that perhaps I should not. She is a distraction. The words come out even with those reservations, almost of their own volition.

"Perhaps Nora can join us," I suggest. "She would make an excellent tour guide."

I see Padraig's eyes sharpen on me. There is no way to suggest bringing Nora on the trip without also displaying my interest in her. I know he is likely filing away the information, perhaps to use against me later, but I have already shown my interest, so I do not fret over it. What is done is done.

"I will ask her if she would like to go," Padraig agrees. "The rover is ready to go now if you would like to gather your things."

"I will go do so now," I agree.

As the only things that I have are the ones I was traveling with, it does not take me long to pack everything up. The scroll always stays with me in any case, so I am in and out of my temporary home in only a few minutes.

When I walk over to the rover, Nora and Errol are already waiting for me beside it. The vehicle itself is quite impressive, the metal gleaming under the Tajss suns.

"If you would like to sit inside, we can be on our way," Errol offers.

"Of course," I agree, nodding at Nora.

She nods back, looking away to slide into the vehicle. Ragnar is already inside, sitting in front and next to Errol. I cannot help but think that they sent two Zmaj with me as guards. That is fine. I have no intention of being violent unless they give me good reason.

Nora herself is a good deterrent. I would not want her to

be accidentally hurt in any confrontation I have. I would never forgive myself.

I enjoy Nora's proximity as we begin our journey, driving out into the desert enclosed in the handy human-constructed mode of transportation. Not only does it save energy because we do not have to traverse the desert on foot, it also provides a level of protection from anything outside. I appreciate that. Still, it is the strangest feeling to move across the desert while sitting comfortably without my legs and wings active.

As we drive, I try not to stare at the lovely object of my attention too much, cognizant of the fact that she is trapped in the vehicle with me, unable to escape. But she keeps her gaze focused outside the window, giving me more than ample opportunity to take in the fine grain of her skin, the gentle variations of color in her hair, the way her cheeks flush when she does turn and notice my attention.

But even when I am looking outside the window or at Nora, I also pay attention to Ragnar and Errol's conversation in front.

"How is the mining settlement doing?"

"They are still not interested in a closer alliance, but I do not think that will last."

Errol shakes his head.

"Perhaps it will. They have shown themselves to be stubborn to a fault, not always having their own best interests at heart. Now they are making noises about renegotiating how much the ores they mine are worth."

"Are they still asking for more use of the rover as well?" Ragnar asks, turning to look at Errol.

"Yes. As is the city. I understand the desire to have the rover more often, but there is only one such vehicle."

Ragnar nods.

"Maybe when they get the invaders' vehicle working properly, that won't be as much of an issue."

"Perhaps. The technical team is working on it in the city with and without me. I cannot be there at all times, not when Kate is with the Tribe."

"Yes," Ragnar agrees. "But I cannot help but think the situation between the mining settlement, the city, and the Tribe is too delicate. Even before we also factor in the meteorite glass."

"Yes. I see what..."

I continue to listen, interested in what they are revealing. There is a whole society being built here, one the Order never even suspected. I am happy for it. It is a much-welcome surprise. But it is not difficult to pick up that there is an uneasy peace among all of these opposing settlements.

Resources are always going to be an issue on Tajss. At least for the foreseeable future. Asteroid ore, ore from wherever these mines are, the rover... They are only the tip of the issue. Food and water, guards against invaders and beasts, not to mention the shelter required to hold strong against the assault of meteorite showers...

Banding together is an excellent idea, but it does not come without stresses of its own. I also find it interesting that they have managed to seize some of the invaders' technology. I applaud their resourcefulness and foresight in that arena.

The journey to the city actually goes by quite fast, less because the journey is short, and more because I am interested in the conversation and am also enjoying being in such close proximity to Nora. I do not know if Errol and Ragnar have forgotten that I am in the back, or if they are deliberately giving me this information to see what I will do with it. Or perhaps they do not think the information is sensitive. We will see, I suppose.

When we do arrive at the city, I am not surprised to see these particular ruins. I know the city is here. I simply have not seen it in years. Have not seen it with the shielding in place and the people actually populating it. When we park the rover and walk outside, I feel a rush of hope at seeing it utilized. It is good to see it with inhabitants. Repairs are obviously underway, though the city is quite large for the population that is apparently currently here, judging by how many people I actually see.

"Let us go see Visidion. I know he is waiting for our arrival," Errol says.

"Can I go see Calista while you do?" Nora asks in that soft voice.

"Of course," Ragnar replies, smiling. "I am certain your friends in the city will be glad to see you."

She smiles in response, the anticipation and excitement in her eyes making them sparkle. The sight is beautiful, but so is everything else about her. With a murmured a goodbye, and a last glance at me, Nora leaves.

"We should be on our way," Errol says once more.

Ragnar nods. So the group of us enters a building, and climbs a staircase to a room, one that appears to be an office.

The Zmaj waiting there for us is clearly the Tribe Commander. I would have known it even if he was the only Zmaj in the room. His presence is commanding, the kind that broadcasts his confidence in himself and his abilities. He also has an aura about him, the kind that draws eyes and attention to him. He is a leader, even if he did not have a group to lead.

As we walk in, his deep emerald eyes take in the group before settling on me. The way he stares at me so deeply makes me wonder if he can see everything that I am keeping to myself, can see that my guard is up against him and everyone else here. It is not true, of course. I know very well that I am not allowing anything I do not want to be seen to be apparent to this male.

"This is Archion," Errol introduces me. "Archion, this is Visidion, the Tribe Commander."

He nods at me.

"I trust you had a comfortable journey?" he asks politely.

"Yes, thank you," I respond, watching as he gives me a thorough scan. I doubt anything escapes his notice.

"I was surprised when I was told the Tribe had run into an unfamiliar Zmaj in the desert. Even more surprised when I learned he helped them defeat the invaders, and two other beasts besides."

"As I am sure you have already been told, I was leading the invaders away from our own encampment. I could not very well leave the group I encountered to fight them alone. Not when there were also females in the group."

Visidion raises a brow.

"There are some who might have left them in any case," he murmurs, cocking his head at me. "I will not ask you more detailed questions. I know I would not answer them if I was attempting to protect my people."

Interesting.

"That is very perceptive of you," I say. "My thanks."

He nods at me, no distress in his eyes. It seems he has some intuition, and it shows him that I pose no threat to him or his people.

"Very well." His gaze turns serious, his voice lowering. "Simply trust this, Archion. Just as you are protecting your people, I will do what is necessary to protect mine."

The threat is clear, but I understand it well.

"That is as I would expect," I respond. And it is. "Rest assured, I have no intention of harming anyone."

"Of course," he agrees, his smile faint. "You may also trust that we will have our eyes upon you." He glances over at Ragnar and Errol. "I am satisfied for now. If he would like to see the city, he is welcome."

"Thank you," I say.

With that endorsement, we leave his office and go outside. The leader is admirable in his own right, the meeting raising my own estimation of the society they are building. Errol and Ragnar show me around the city briefly, though only the main points that I would have guessed anyway. I know they are still wary of my observing anything important or sensitive, and I cannot blame them.

After the brief tour, we take the time to eat at one of the areas dedicated for it, encountering other Zmaj and humans eating there as well. We also find Nora there with a group of human females, friends she has in the city.

I watch as she throws her head back and laughs at something one of them says. She is glowing with happiness. I am glad I requested her presence. She is obviously enjoying herself.

We do not stay in the city long once our original reason for being here is done. Nora did not act as much of a guide, but that is not why I wanted her to come anyway. After we eat, Ragnar and Errol usher us back to the waiting rover.

On the journey back to the Tribe, I decide to finally actively interact with Nora. It is a wonder how much we have said to each other with glances while we have never had a real conversation. It is time to change that.

She is once again looking out the window, remaining in her small bubble of silence.

"The female you sat next to during the meal, she was your friend Calista?" I start. A safe foray.

Nora starts somewhat at my voice, glancing over at me before looking away again.

"Yes," she murmurs. "The others were friends I've made in the city."

I nod, wanting to know more. Wanting to know everything.

"How did you come to be with the Tribe?" I ask, taking a different tack. "How did everyone come to live together in this manner?"

She pauses, as if thinking how to respond properly.

"The others have their own stories," she murmurs. "I and the rest of my group are actually a newer addition to both the city and the Tribe."

"A newer addition?" I repeat, confused. "How did this occur? Were you not on the same ship?"

"We were in a separate scouting vessel," she explains. "When the main ship was attacked and crash-landed on Tajss, we landed further away." A shadow crosses her face. Clearly the memories of that time are not good ones. I regret asking her a question that makes her unhappy, but I still want the answer. Still want to understand everything I can about her. Everything that has made her what she is. "We sustained casualties, mainly from guster attacks."

My stomach clenches at the thought of her and the other delicate human females being attacked by those vicious creatures.

"Guster attacks? How did you survive?"

"We were rescued by a Zmaj warrior," she explains, smiling slightly. "Gomul is Bashir's father. If it was not for him, taking us back to his underground tunnels, offering us a place to take shelter, his protection, and food...we likely would not have survived for very long at all."

I shake my head wonderingly.

"How long were you in these tunnels?" I ask. "Before you came here."

"Years," she says quietly. "We would still be there now if it wasn't for Kate. Or Annabel even, I suppose. If Annabel had been a better leader, Kate would not have rebelled and taken us with her."

"A group of you left the tunnels to cross the desert alone?"

I ask incredulously. That sounds ridiculously dangerous for people so ill equipped.

She grins, her eyes twinkling at me. I feel my breath catch at that expression, aimed at me for the first time. I want to make her smile like that more often.

"We did," she says proudly, raising her adorable chin. "But Kate is the one who built the rover, so we weren't on foot. We rode across the desert, hoping to find something, anything else. And that's when we ran into Errol."

"Ah," I say, my face clearing. "And he brought you back to the Tribe."

"To the city," Nora corrects. "When Kate returned with him to the Tribe, I decided to go with them. The city is great, but the Tribe feels more like family, more like a home."

I nod. I can see what she means. The city was impressive, but it did not have the same sense of a tightly knit community the Tribe does. Everyone feels more separated. Part of that is simply because there is more room there.

"What of the rest of your group?" I ask, curious. "Those still in the tunnels?"

She shakes her head, frowning.

"We told them about the city, about the Tribe. And about the epis. The epis was the real game changer—I didn't even realize how terrible I felt until I took it. We're just not built for this climate here." She sighs, shaking her head. "But Annabel wouldn't budge, even after Kate told them everything. She hates Rosalind—the woman in charge in the city—and she would rather lead in that terrible place rather than leave it. And I guess the other women there aren't strong enough to leave on their own. Or maybe they're just scared to. I don't know."

I can see the flash of sadness cross her face at the thought of the other females. Her heart is tender indeed. I want to reach out and pull her close, offer her comfort. However, I am afraid I will not stop there. Nora is innocent, I dare not advance upon her even for such an innocent matter, for fear that my restraint may give way before I have chance to ask permission from my Order.

So I offer her what comfort I can through my words.

"Perhaps they will come to their senses with time," I murmur. "There are times when people must reach the correct conclusion themselves. Nobody can convince them."

She nods, turning to look out the window again.

"Maybe," she agrees in a low voice.

We move on to lighter conversation topics after that. But rather than the tension dissipating, it only grows between us. An attraction, a knowing. Whatever it is, it grows stronger every time I see her.

Upon reaching the Tribe, we are both polite with one another, but there is no denying the friction of awareness between us, the tension. When she steps out of the rover, she forgets her pack.

"Oh, my pack," she mutters, turning back.

I hold it out for her, stepping out as well.

"Thank you," she murmurs, her hand grazing mine as she takes the pack.

A fever of need flows through me even at that light touch. When her cheeks flush and she raises her eyes to meet my own, I am certain she is affected too. The knowledge only makes me burn hotter. Nora is a test that I do not know if I have the strength to pass. It is humbling indeed.

We have time to clean up and rest from our journey before it is time for the communal dinner. The mood is light and happy, a drink that they call "wine" being passed around to keep up the communal spirits. I drink the beverage, speaking to the other Zmaj as my eye returns to Nora.

"Where is Nora? I'm in the mood to hear her sing," Delilah asks in a slightly loud voice.

My eye already on Nora, I watch as she attempts to slink away without notice. But Delilah sees the movement and finds her before she is out of sight.

"Nora! Don't leave yet—you have to sing for everyone!"

Nora turns back reluctantly, her cheeks flushed. It is clear she is embarrassed, her desire to stay in the background making itself known. She possesses a humility that she does not truly need. She is so much more than she realizes.

I have ever been more enchanted with a woman. Perhaps too enchanted. I know I'm so completely enraptured with her that I would lose control of myself if another claimed her. My bijass would rise from within and overtake any discipline I have worked so hard to build.

Caught, Nora does not attempt to run out again. Instead, her eyes drift over the assembled crowd.

I watch.

She is mine.

When her eyes find my own, our gazes lock. I can hear her heart skip a beat, so I know she is aware of what she is to me as well. On some level of her human psyche, she knows that she is mine. Her cheeks darken more as she blushes a lovely deep pink, but she does not look away. Her eyes hold my own boldly for a moment, as if to draw strength.

And then the she opens her mouth to sing. My own hearts skip a beat in response, the sound coming from her so beautiful it would make a grown dragon cry. Inside of course.

My eyes remain trained on her as she continues, the dulcet tones winding around the crowd. Not looking away even for a moment. I am aware I could be giving away my intent to others, my feelings, but I could not tear away my own gaze if I tried.

When she finishes the song, there is a moment of stunned

silence. Followed by a roar of approval. A justified sound if I have ever heard one.

Almost immediately, others pick up instruments and begin to play music, everyone coming together to dance. The wine is flowing freely, the mood joyous. I am tempted to ask Nora to dance with me as well, but when I turn back towards her, it is to see the small dragonlings holding her hands and pulling her away, giggling happily as they do.

Ah. She is once again making a swift escape from the social pressures that plagues her so. My heart fills with a glowing warmth at the sight of her leading the young ones away. She would make an excellent mother. That much is abundantly clear.

I do not stay much longer to enjoy the festivities. Without Nora there as well, they lose their appeal.

But when I make my way back to my cave, it is to find a restless night waiting for me. My sleep is fitful at best, my thoughts lingering on her and only her.

Nora.

Even in my dreams, it is she who haunts me.

## 9

### NORA

"Nora! Nora—the guards are telling us to come outside!"

I jerk out of a sound sleep at Delilah's urgent voice. Sitting up in bed, I look over at the mouth of my cave.

"What?" I ask groggily.

"The guards are saying there's something in the sky that we have to see," Delilah explains further, already backing out. "Come on!" she urges as she lets the curtain drop back into place.

Something in the sky? I throw back the covers and slip my shoes onto my feet, hurrying outside too. Being on high alert all the time because of the invaders, my first thought is that we're under attack somehow.

But if that was the case, why would the guards tell us all to come outside? To look up at the sky? Wouldn't they tell us to take cover instead of coming out into the open?

Hurrying out with the rest of the Tribe, curiosity beats at me and everyone else. I hear the same questions voiced by the crowd moving with me.

"What do they want us to see?"

"Are we under attack?"

"I don't think so. They didn't tell us to bring our shock sticks..."

That's true. We burst out into the open, joining the others already gathered, their heads tilted back to look up at the sky. I look up too, slowing to a stop as I do.

"Oh!" I exclaim softly. "Oh, wow."

"You got that right," Fallon mutters from beside me, her eyes also glued to the sky above.

I can see now why the guards wanted us all to come out to see what they were seeing. The night sky is lit up with streams of multicolored lights, a dream of hazy colors. Gentle greens, lavenders, oranges and reds. Like a fairy tale come to life. The ribbons of color aren't opaque, but somewhat transparent and blurred, starlight peeking through them. They move across the sky, ripples of gorgeous hues.

Beautiful. There is no other way to describe the sight. Everyone is quiet as we take in nature's show. Even the children, awakened for the occasion. They watch with wide eyes. It must not be a common occurrence even for the Zmaj or they would not have had us come out to look. Sometimes I'm less in the know than the other humans, living underground as we did during the first leg of our time here on Tajss.

I would never have guessed in those tunnels, under Annabel's hard leadership, that there would be something this beautiful to look forward to on Tajss. That I would find some meaning in my life here rather than just struggling to survive.

I could stand there and stare up at that pretty sky all night. Unfortunately, even as I think that, it's like I've jinxed the show.

More-familiar glowing, fiery streaks appear in the sky. At

this point, we all know exactly what they are, but one of the guards yells it out anyway.

"Meteorite shower! Everyone back inside!"

We start hustling back in, the conversation starting up once more as we do.

"Do you think the glass might be different in the morning?"

"Maybe. What if it's colorful?"

"What if it doesn't make glass? What if the meteors are different?"

I can hear the excitement in the voices at the prospect of the meteorite shower producing something new this time.

But I just can't get excited. I feel shaken now that the pretty picture is out of sight. Maybe because there's just been so much change. I'm a little tired of always feeling on edge, wondering what's going to come. How we're going to deal with it.

What's wrong with routine? At this point that's what I really want.

I could appreciate the beauty of the lights, but I sure could do without the uncertainty around what they mean. If anything.

Once back under the shelter of the cave system, some people mill about wanting to discuss things, but I return to my little cave and my messy pallet. I'd rather not rehash things I always worry about anyway.

Sleep is a little more difficult to find this time, but eventually I calm back down enough to drift off. When I wake up the next morning, I wonder what the day will bring. But everything seems normal enough as I have breakfast and ready myself for the day.

The first thing I do is check in on the dragonlings. The bags under Mei's eyes and her generally unkempt appearance tell me something is wrong before she says a word.

"What is it?" I ask right away.

"It's Ganeese. He's been running a fever all night," she explains.

"Oh no!" I exclaim softly, looking over her shoulder to see him curled up in bed still.

He's usually up earlier than everyone. I go over to him, touching the back of my hand to his forehead and finding it feverish. His eyes open at the touch. He looks up at me, blinking. His gaze is little dull, his normal energy definitely lower than usual.

"Nora," he says in a husky voice, brightening slightly. "Are you staying?"

"Sure, baby," I murmur, taking his soft little hand in my own. I turn to Mei. "Why don't you catch a nap, maybe grab some food. I can watch over him for a bit."

"Are you sure?" she asks.

"Of course. Now go—if I were you I would take the opportunity to close my eyes."

She smiles a little, nodding her head.

"I'm not going to refuse," she agrees. "Okay, I'm going to take a quick nap, have some breakfast. I'll be back soon though, okay?"

"Take your time," I urge.

She comes over and kisses her son on the forehead.

"Is it okay if Nora watches you for a little while?" she asks.

"Okay," Ganeese agrees easily. "But you'll be back soon?"

I know he's sick for sure then. He usually doesn't have a whole lot of separation anxiety, not when he knows I'm going to be the one watching him.

"Yes. In just a little while," she reassures him.

With one last thank you thrown at me, Mei leaves to try to get some shut-eye.

"Can you tell me a story?" Ganeese asks groggily.

"Of course," I murmur, smoothing his hair back from his forehead. "There once was an ogre in a faraway land—"

"What color was the ogre?"

"Green."

"Was he big or small?"

I chuckle a little.

"He was big. Maybe not really tall, but at least sufficiently wide."

I hold my arms out to demonstrate. He nods, his eyes half closing again now that he has a firm picture in his mind.

"Okay. You can keep going now."

"Why, thank you," I say wryly, laughing. "Anyway, this ogre lived far away from everybody else..."

I expect him to fall asleep quickly, but his eyes stay open, focused on my face as I speak. I stretch the story out to make it last, embellishing parts, making sounds that I know will make him laugh.

It's most likely been about an hour when I notice a shadow at the door. When I look over, my eyes meet Archion's. He nods at me, but stays just outside the cave opening, politely listening and waiting for me to finish. Slightly more self-conscious now that I know he's listening, I try to refocus on the story.

Why is he here? What does he want to talk to me about? I try to keep going, but I keep losing my train of thought, my eye going back to Archion.

I finally give up and start wrapping up the story when Mei comes back in, looking a little more rested, her hair combed back and a new set of clothes on her body.

"Thank you so much, Nora," she says, hugging me tight. "You can head out now though—it looks like Archion wants to speak with you."

I nod, standing.

"Get better soon, munchkin," I murmur, leaning down to kiss Ganeese's forehead.

"Bye, Nora!" he murmurs, his eyes opening slightly before closing once more. Fighting off sleep like always.

Taking a deep breath, I rub my palms on my pants, trying to calm my nerves. Archion watches me approach, straightening from where he's been leaning against the wall. I walk all the way out before I turn towards him, making sure I'm at least out of line of sight.

"Sorry to keep you waiting."

He shakes his head.

"No apology necessary. Is the child feeling better?"

I shrug.

"He's sick, but it doesn't seem too bad. Hopefully a day or two of rest will fix him right up."

He nods.

"You are very good with children," he observes, his eyes softening.

I shrug again, not knowing what to say to that as I shove my hands into my pockets. Like a child myself. But compliments are kind of hard for me to take usually. Barring my cooking.

Trying to forge past the awkwardness, I asked him why he sought me out.

"We have been asked to join the collection team," he explains. "The meteors are emanating a strange light, and Errol seems keen to come into possession of the material before the invaders potentially disrupt the scene."

I nod—that makes sense.

"Okay. Is everyone getting ready to go now?"

"Yes. We are supposed to be leaving soon."

I follow him out to the wall, seeing a group already assembled there, Errol standing in front.

He's giving everyone a talk.

"...there have been less-frequent meteorite showers. It is one of the reasons I want to go look so quickly," he explains to the gathered group. "We need to get to any and all material we can while it is still there, before the invaders could potentially get to it. We do not know if the time between each shower will continue to lengthen, or if the showers will cease altogether."

"How will we fuel the shields and shock sticks if the showers stop?" one of the women asks from the crowd.

"That is a concern," Errol agrees. "But all we are in control of at the moment is gathering as much of the material as we can while it is available. And, perhaps, these meteors will offer something more impressive this time." He looks around at each of us. "As always, stay near enough to each other to call for help and keep watch on your surroundings. I am certain we are not the only ones who noticed the shower. Or the difference in the sky last night. I hope we reach the material without trouble, but we must be prepared if we do not."

I hear everybody murmur their agreement around me as my heartbeat picks up pace once more. I know I'm not the bravest person. But no matter how much I try to lessen my fear, my mind still just always goes back to everything that can go wrong. Guster, zemlja, invaders... The list goes on.

When I turn away from Errol, it's to find Archion watching me once more, his gaze sharp, incisive. Why do I always feel like he knows exactly what I'm thinking? His next words don't dispel that notion, fanciful though it might be.

"With me, you are safe. I will guard you with my life," he reassures me in his low, sure voice. A charge goes through me at the intensity of his gaze, his words.

I believe him. And isn't that crazy? My heart picks up even more, the heat in my cheeks letting me know that I'm blushing again and failing to hide it. I feel like I spend ninety percent of my time around him blushing.

All I can manage is a smile as the heat flows through me, as my heart softens at the care in his words, in his demeanor. I look down once more, cursing my shyness. I don't know how much longer I can take this little dance between us.

And I'm growing tired of worrying that I might be imagining it.

10

ARCHION

*W*e travel out to the area we estimate the asteroids hit last night.

Once we are near the area and we have had a chance to scout for any danger, Errol begins to divide the group further, into human and Zmaj couples. It appears as though everyone was expecting this. Perhaps that is a common way to split the group.

"And Nora, you and Archion are paired as well." Nora and I glance at each other, neither of us surprised. We are the only ones left. "With the carts we now have, it should be a simpler task this time, at least to transport anything we find back to the Tribe. Bring back anything you find that you think is from the meteorite shower. They may have produced more than simple meteorite glass." He glances around the group. "And if you need help, yell out. We must all remain within audible distance of each other."

Everybody voices their agreement with that plan.

From my understanding, the new carts that we have pushed out this far with us were forged by hand from the excess metals acquired from the invaders' ship. They will

82

most definitely make transporting larger amounts of anything a simpler task.

"If nobody has any further questions, we may split and search the sand," Errol continues, having to raise his voice over the wind. "We must hurry—I do not want to stay out here longer than necessary. For multiple reasons."

When nobody speaks up, he nods sharply.

"Everyone move towards your section."

Nora and I turn towards the left, expanding out in the rough circle Errol decided upon. We should be able to find everything in this formation.

As we walk, I keep a careful eye on Nora. The farther away we have traveled from the Tribe's cave system, the stronger the winds have become. Until our hair is whipping out in front of our faces, tugging at our clothing. Nora continues to wear a brave face, tucking her hair behind her ears in an effort to clear her vision. She is clearly out of her element here. Though this brutal wind is not comfortable for me either.

We scour the ground, searching for the pits that indicate the areas where the meteors have hit. The whole time, I am paying as much attention to Nora as I am to searching for what we came for. I stay near her, within a leap's distance. The winds are gaining speed fast, the sand beginning to lift from the ground.

I look up, squinting at the force of the air. Sand is rising all around us. When I look farther out into the distance, I see a wall of it barreling towards us.

I begin to hear yells in the distance. The words are muffled and unclear, but the alarm in them is not at all difficult to discern. As the sand begins to scour my skin, I turn towards Nora, ready to tell her we must leave, must find shelter.

At that moment, she stumbles and then begins to rise.

Stomach clenching, I leap towards her, fighting through the buffeting wind to wrap my arms around her delicate frame just as she starts to slide down the dune, the wind too strong. She is too light now to remain anchored on the ground. We will not be making the meteorite landing sites anytime soon.

She looks up at me, the fear and bewilderment in her gaze tugging at me.

I must keep her safe.

Acting quickly, I scoop her into my arms, spreading my wings and curving them around to cover her. The sand is now hitting us hard enough that I fear it will damage her soft skin. She clings to me, tucking her head in against my chest and closing her eyes against the sand.

I close my eyes as much as I can without completely compromising my vision, walking into the storm. I have not felt this level of fear in some time, and I know it is due to the precious burden I carry. I cannot allow harm to come to Nora. I use that fear to drive me. Closing my eyes, I take shallow breaths with my head bent towards my chest, attempting to keep my airways clear.

I must focus on my inner knowing—a difficult task within the edges of the sandstorm. But the knowledge that I must keep Nora safe forces a calm over me. I fall into that near meditative state, reaching for to the quiet voice within. The voice that lets me see beyond what I can see with my eyes alone.

Sensitive to everything Tajss can tell me now, I follow a sense that I cannot quite name. Pushing against the wind, I hold on tightly to its suggestions. I must trust that it will lead me to whatever sanctuary can be had in the storm of weather now besetting us. Every step I move forward is a fight, the wind too strong for me to use my wings to glide, even if I did not need them to keep Nora safe.

Soon, I cannot see farther than one stride in front of me. Eventually, even that much visibility must be compromised in order for me to keep my eyes safe. They already feel raw from having them open even a slit.

Urgency and fear swirl within me, but I keep the emotions at bay, focusing on that sense that draws me forward. I cannot stop. I must keep going. Tajss will not disappoint me, will not lead me astray.

I am so focused on pushing myself forward, on fighting the wind and the pain of the sand scraping against my skin, that I do not realize I am near an obstruction until my wings scrape against hot rock.

I pause, reaching a foot out to feel. It is rock, but it does not provide much cover, at least not here. I slowly sidle over to my right, using my wings and my foot to feel the way.

The wind is so strong now that I stumble more than once, keeping my grip on Nora tight. There must be somewhere here that we can take cover. I keep moving, refusing to give up, refusing to leave hope behind. Gritting my teeth, I continued to inch towards the side.

Searching. Until my foot hits nothing. Not waiting for any more of an indication, I surge forward. The painful scrape of the sand ceases abruptly. My breathing is harsh in the relative quiet, the wind no longer howling directly into my ears.

Safe.

We are safe.

I take a moment simply to take a deep breath, coughing immediately as I do.

Nora stirs in my arms.

"Archion?"

I shake my head, bending over to set her on her feet as I cough out sand.

"Here, let me help."

I feel a soft cloth brushing over my eyes, clearing away the sand that has gathered there.

After a few moments of recovery, I can finally take a breath, standing upright again. Nora draws closer to me, looking up at me in concern.

"Are you okay?"

I nod, looking around. It is a shallow cave, if a space this small can be called a cave. It only goes a few strides into the rock face I felt with my foot.

A particularly strong gust of the wind howls directly outside the opening we just came in from. Nora starts next to me, her hand coming out to grip my forearm as she draws closer. I turn to her, wrapping an arm around her shoulders.

"Do not fear. We will be safe here."

She nods, her eyes still on the sandstorm outside as she draws closer, her body pressing against the side of mine. Even in this situation, I feel myself tense at the softness of her. She feels that subtle shift in me, her gaze darting up to look at my face.

I know my eyes broadcast the desire I feel for her, the want that I have been struggling with ever since I first saw her.

Her gaze immediately drops, her cheeks flushed. Even the shyness is appealing to me.

Turning away, she shrugs off her pack and opens it up, crouching to upend the contents onto the ground.

"We should figure out how much we have with us and how much we'll need," she offers, still not looking at me, deliberately turning her attention to the rations to avoid the sexual tension between us.

I feel my hearts soften.

Patience. I will hold on to patience for her.

I crouch too, sifting through what she has laid out before

upending my own pack and looking through it as well. There is not much.

The bulk of the meat we have brought along is in a compartment in the cart we were forced to abandon. Nora sees exactly what I do.

"It's not enough. Not if we have to stay here for a while," she says, panic starting to thread through her voice. "We definitely don't have enough water to get through more than today."

I stare at her face, drinking in her pure, unwittingly sensual beauty even as I reach for the words to help calm her, to be the voice of reason we need.

"Anything we do not have can be hunted. Do your best to relax, to remain calm."

I ensure my voice is measured, slow and relaxed to help her. She shudders slightly, her shoulders dropping as she nods.

"Okay. Okay, you're right," she says. "Panic won't help anything."

I nod as she gathers our resources back into our respective packs. As I watch her, I realize just how vulnerable she is here on Tajss. Not only is she small and soft, if we came across invaders or a beast rather than a simple sandstorm...

I feel that clench of fear once more. It is unacceptable that she is so completely vulnerable.

I glance outside. The storm appears to be stronger, gaining momentum rather than losing it. We will likely have to spend at least the following day here. I immediately resolve to make good use of our enforced time here.

Tomorrow, I will teach Nora how to fight.

## 11

## NORA

*I* pull myself together as I ready my pallet so I can lie down.

The sandstorm was completely disorienting, but now that I've had a moment to take a breath, I feel a lot more calm. To be honest, I know it's mostly because of Archion. And not just because he was able to find this shelter for us. How he did it with no visibility, I have no idea. It's kind of a miracle to me.

But he also helped by just being him.

He's a true rock under pressure, someone I could fully lean on. I know for a fact that if I'd been alone, I would have freaked out way more. But his calm, steady energy and his reassuring words help me pull back from that edge of pure, unadulterated panic.

I'm so glad he's with me.

After smoothing down the top, I lie on the pallet, my eye going to Archion once more. He's rolling out his own pallet between mine and the cave's opening, which I'm sure is no mistake. I've seen him put himself between danger and others too many times now. He's just that kind of person, down to the core.

It's ridiculously attractive. Maybe that's my lizard brain talking, wanting a male who can protect me, but it doesn't change how I feel.

I watch his calm face for a moment before tracing lower down on his body to the muscles of his arms, which are bunching in an eye-catching way as he finishes up the simple task. Just the sight of him settles me inside, makes feel more secure. Maybe it's stupid to think so, but I can't help but feel that no harm will come to me under Archion's protection. For now, I'm more than happy to take it.

Exhausted from the trip so far, the sandstorm, and the anxiety attack after seeing how much we don't have in terms of supplies, my eyes start to close of their own accord while I watch him. I don't try to fight it.

Might as well catch as much sleep as I can before we have to go out and brave the sands again. It's not like there's anything else we can do until the wind dies down. Sleep is the most productive thing I can think of. I don't know when I actually succumb completely, but I sink deeper into sleep than I expect to be able to under the circumstances. Maybe because I know Archion is right there to watch over me. Nobody has ever made me feel this safe.

Unfortunately, I don't get to stay in that welcome slumber. My eyes snap open in alarm as the covers are jerked off my body. What the hell?

"Wake up, Nora. We have much to accomplish today."

Huh? I blink up at Archion's much-too-awake face. Nuh uh. No way. I groan, closing my eyes and rolling over onto my stomach to bury my face in the pallet once more.

"No we don't," I respond grumpily. "I can still hear the wind outside."

"It is not nearly as strong as it was yesterday," he retorts.

I don't respond. Maybe if I'm quiet he'll take the hint and just go away so I can sink back into that delicious—

I squeak as the pallet tilts under me, sending me tumbling right off onto the hard ground. I glare up at Archion, shoving my hair off my face. He's still gripping the edge of my bed.

"Why won't you let me sleep!" I growl, looking over at the mouth of the cave. Dawn's light is just barely breaking through from what I can see. "The suns aren't even up yet!"

Archion just chuckles, looking annoyingly bright-eyed and bushy-tailed.

"There is no time to wait. A threat can catch you unawares no matter how early."

"Huh?" I draw my knees up and rest my head against them, closing my eyes again. "This is way too early to be doing this much talking."

"No, it is not. If anything, it is much too late for you to learn how to defend yourself."

That has me raising my head, frowning up at him as the fog slowly starts to slip from my brain. Grudgingly, but relentlessly. I am so not a morning person. It takes me a while to get out of bed even at a reasonable time.

"Defend myself?" I ask.

He nods, crossing his arms. Now that I'm more awake, the bulge of his biceps does distract me some. I'm not proud of it, but it is what it is. I might as well enjoy something if I have to be up this early.

"You are soft, but not defenseless. With some training, you will not be such an easy target."

I might have taken offense at the easy target remark if it wasn't so true. Training. I rub my eyes, trying to digest his words.

"You want to train me?" I ask, just to be sure. "In self-defense?"

"Yes. You should have been trained some time ago. The fact that you are still so vulnerable is unconscionable."

I mean...I can't argue with that either.

But...

"I've never been good at physical things," I venture hesitantly. "I don't know how well I'll take to whatever you have in mind."

He shakes his head.

"Everything can be improved upon, no matter the starting point. And you have never had me to help you before." I admire his confidence, I guess. "Come. We will now begin."

I don't think I'm going to be able to get out of this.

"Fine," I grumble, admitting defeat. Rising to my feet, I look for my shoes. "One sec."

The last thing I want to do right now the get out of the pallet and exercise. But he's right. If this training can inch me towards feeling less helpless, more confident in my own abilities, that could only be a good thing So I'll force myself to do it. Never mind the fact that he's forcing me anyway.

"First, we shall run," he announces as soon as my shoes are on.

"Run?" I groan, hoping I heard him wrong. "Isn't the wind too strong for that?"

He shakes his head, turning towards the cave opening.

"No, it has slowed enough for us to run. But we will tie cloths around our mouths and noses just in case, to avoid breathing in any dust."

He has an answer for everything, doesn't he?

Dubious, but ready to at least try it, I take a scrap of cloth that I used to wrap the rations and tie it around the bottom half of my face instead. Like a cowboy ready to rob a moving train. At least there's nobody around to see how ridiculous we look.

When we step outside, I have to admit, at least to myself,

that I see what Archion means. The wind isn't nearly as strong as it was when we first stumbled into this cave. Maybe not weak enough yet to find the others or to travel back to the Tribe, but a run might be doable. Damn.

"How do we make sure we don't get lost?" I ask, raising my voice now that we're outside.

It's still kind of loud. There's also still dust in the air, enough to obscure things at any kind of distance.

"We will run around the rock," Archion explains, pitching his voice loud enough for me to hear. "There is no way we will lose ourselves that way."

That makes sense. With that brief reply, he takes off in front of me.

"Come, Nora!" he calls over his shoulder.

Sighing, I push myself forward through the sand. Nothing like a good old morning jog to get the adrenaline going. I make sure to keep Archion in my sight—which is easy enough since he's deliberately slowing down so I can keep up at all—and the rock face to my left so I don't get lost.

It's really hard at first. I can't even remember how long it's been since I've run. Well, at least not for exercise. There's been a couple of times there now where we've been in the meteorite shower or a battle situation where I've had to move quick. Huh. Maybe I should have started cardiovascular conditioning much earlier.

After going for a few more minutes, I realize all over again why I didn't. Running sucks.

"I hate this so much," I grumble to myself.

I try to keep it under my breath, but Archion's bat ears hear me. Slowing so he's next to me rather than in front of me, he looks over.

"It is only because you are just beginning," he offers. "You will strengthen with practice."

I roll my eyes. "Maybe," I humor him.

Do I really want to practice this torture enough so I'm better at it? Ugh. I force myself to keep going. No way am I quitting this early. And, surprisingly, after a few more minutes, I actually hit a rhythm. The blood starts coursing through my body in a rush and my heart settles into the new pace. I break out in a sweat that's different from the one that's only due to the desert heat. It actually feels kind of good. I feel...alive. Okay. Maybe Archion wasn't totally wrong.

We still run for longer than I would have liked to, but I'm not grumbling anymore by the time we complete the circuit and reach the cave again. Inside, I walk to get my heart rate down, tearing off the makeshift mask to gulp in deep breaths. But even though I'm tired, I feel stronger than before the run. Huh. Who would have thought?

"We will eat now," Archion tells me, rummaging through the rations. "Then we will begin training with the electro-stick."

I nod. Sounds good to me so long as it isn't more running. Once I catch my breath, I have some water and eat a light breakfast. I don't want to weigh myself down too much if I'm going to have to keep moving. If I have to throw up in front of Archion... Yeah, I'd really rather not.

"Ready?" he asks as soon as I stand up.

"Yes."

He grabs the stick and tosses it to me.

I fumble a little but manage to catch it.

"Your goal is to be able to defend yourself," he begins, already circling me with his lochaber. "That is what we will focus on. Perhaps, as you improve, you may learn more offensive techniques."

"Okay."

He's right. I'm not going to be the first line of offense unless something has gone terribly wrong.

"But first, I need to assess your current skill level. I am going to attack and you have to do your best to defend yourself. Attack me in return if you have the chance." He gives me a moment, bracing his own feet. "Ready?"

"Not really."

He smiles slightly.

"In some instances, true readiness is not going to be found."

I sigh.

"All right. Let's do it."

He attacks before the last word is out. He's fast. Real fast. And my performance is poor. Though even calling it poor is being nice. I get tapped by that damn lochaber every time he attacks, I stumble over my own feet, and at one point I even drop my electro-stick altogether. It's at that point that he stops, stepping back.

Then he nods.

"You know nothing," he states, completely matter-of-fact. "We will start with the basics."

It stings, but he's not wrong. I do know nothing.

"I'm ready," I say, trying to set my ego aside.

That was pretty embarrassing, and I don't think the embarrassing portion of events is exactly over.

"Good. Here is how you should hold the stick for blocking. And here is how you should hold the stick for striking, depending upon what type of strike you would like to accomplish."

I listen intently, watching the positioning of his hands. When I try to mimic him, he watches, correcting as he needs to. When he's satisfied with the placement of my hands, he nods sharply, stepping back once more.

"Good. Now we will go over defensive blocks and also how to move your feet to avoid blows altogether. Since you are so small, it would be best to avoid blows rather than attempt to absorb the force." That makes a lot of sense. "Ready?"

I nod, my heart already beating faster.

"Yes."

He doesn't hold back, at least not in speed. He flips the lochaber around, and then he lunges at me with the blunt end. I try to block and move out of the way at the same time, succeeding only in stumbling into the blow. Not that it is much of a blow. He only taps me, obviously in full control of his weapon even though he is moving so quickly. I feel my face redden, but he doesn't look at all fazed.

"You are not accustomed to being in a true fight. That is fine. Much of this training will simply be helping you reach that mindset," he explains. "Now. If I were to attack you in the same manner once more, you should move your feet like this."

He comes over to my side and moves over smoothly, towards where the outside of his body would be rather than towards the center. I watch him and mimic the movement. I'm not as smooth or fast, but it is roughly the same move.

"Very good," he praises. "If you're not quite fast enough, as you move, also block with your shock stick like this."

I watch him carefully, a little more aware of my weakness as I attempt to move in the same way that he does. Now that I've been embarrassed and moved on, I'm not in my head as much, which helps.

"Yes, good!" he praises me once more. "Now, if you are quick enough to move away from the blow, and your attacker is extended in this manner, then you should take advantage and use the stick against their unprotected side. Using the end to stun is ideal, but even a blow will hurt." He lunges towards the invisible opponent. "Understand?"

"I think so."

"Good. Now I will attempt to attack you once more."

I take a deep breath, adjusting my grip on my electro-stick. My heart is pounding now. He doesn't give me any warning, which I'm not expecting at all. Letting out an embarrassing squeak, I jump back, leaving myself wide open for a tap to the midsection. He doesn't get angry, but rather chuckles, shaking his head. It's almost worse.

"Be alert!" he barks, almost goading, moving back once more. "Your opponents will not give you warning before they attack. Be ready!"

Okay. Be ready. Fine. He attacks me again. I don't execute well again.

"Come, Nora! It is time for you to seize your 'girl power' as the other females say!" he shouts as he continues to attack me, not stopping this time.

I scowl at him, irritated. Where the hell did he hear that?

"I'll show you girl power," I mutter.

He smiles at my anger.

"Use it," he orders.

He's right. I try to channel that irritation, that frustration. He attacks again. And again. Drilling the movement into my brain. Until he lunges at me and I move smoothly, my body shifting and flowing. I don't know how it looks, but every-thing feels exactly right. I even manage to tap him with the tip of the electro-stick, mock shocking him.

When he steps back this time, he has a wide grin on his face.

"Very good!"

I'm breathing hard while he isn't even out of breath yet. But I don't care. I did it! I feel myself glowing at the praise even though it's such a minor thing I've just learned. It took effort anyway.

"Now, I will alternate sides. You need to be ready for this kind of attack from every angle."

I nod and quickly learn that it's a whole other ballgame to

go in another direction. It should be intuitive shouldn't it? But it really, really isn't. When I get whacked for the third time, I growl.

"Use it!" he pushes me again. "A tantrum will not help—use every emotion you feel!"

"It's easy to say when you're not the one being whacked!" I snarl back.

He only laughs and attacks once more. I have to get my shit together fast, or risk being whacked again and again. He keeps going, his body apparently tireless, until I'm so irritated at being whacked I start to move better, start to actually block and avoid strikes.

When I manage to avoid three in a row, he steps back again to give me a reprieve.

"Very good!" he repeats again. "Now, we will try something more challenging. A bladed weapon has to be treated differently than a blunt end. I have been using the blunt end this entire time but I want you to imagine that it is a blade. Also, a weapon is not always used. Sometimes you will have to deal with a larger opponent attacking you with his body alone. That requires a different defensive technique."

I listen intently, watching him as he takes my electro-stick and shows me how he wants me to move my hands and my feet.

"And remember—your goal is to keep your body safe. If that means compromising your electro-stick, so be it. It is not ideal, because without your weapon you are much more vulnerable. However, do not hold on to it to the detriment of your own safety. Understand?"

"Yes."

I'm completely focused at this point, and I feel the moves coming a little easier—as if the base level is being built upon. Which I guess is exactly what's happening.

"Good. Now, I am going to go slow at first, attacking you

in a manner that will require you to defend and attack using every one of the techniques I just showed you. Once you demonstrate you can do them all slowly, I will increase the pace again."

Wait.

"Why didn't you do that before? You went at me at full speed from the beginning!"

"I did not attack you at full speed. You would have no chance to block or attack. But I did attack you faster than I'm going to now. Why?" He grins. "Because it was fun," he says, shrugging his shoulders.

I narrow my eyes at him.

"Fun?" I snarl.

"Yes." When he sees my brows lower and my grip tighten on my electro-stick, his grin only widens. "Use it."

The sound I make is not at all pretty. Oh man, I think I want to punch him in the face the next time he says that. I try to shake off the thought, to focus.

At least he does go slower, just like he said he would. Still, I'm scrambling to apply everything he taught me, even at half speed, and I'm being whacked again and again once more.

Every time I make a mistake, he stops and shows me what I should have done, which I appreciate. We go through it again. And again. And again. Until I start to get the hang of it. It isn't pretty, but I am doing the moves. As soon as I have a fair grasp, he increases the speed, and I'm back to being whacked all over again.

"Damn it!" I mutter as he taps my hip.

"You are improving," he encourages me, stepping back. "These are intermediate techniques. You have graduated from the beginning ones very quickly. You should be proud."

I rub my head.

"It might be easier to be proud if I wasn't getting hit all the time," I point out.

He smiles, the edges softer. "Perhaps. But then you would not be improving as quickly as you are."

I guess he has me there. And I'm actually really grateful that he's teaching me all this. It's unlikely that I'll need to fight on my own, but I feel a hell of a lot less vulnerable now with a few moves under my belt.

Maybe I can't fight Archion and win, but maybe that's not a fair standard, considering that most of the Zmaj I know couldn't fight Archion and win.

However, at the minimum, I can have the ability to stop attackers flat, assuming I remember all of this. And assuming the electro-stick has enough juice.

As my confidence has grown over the last few hours, I've started to wonder what else I can do.... What else I'm capable of.

"Come," Archion orders, turning me towards our pallets, the only place to sit here. "You have earned a break. We will eat, drink, and bathe."

"Bathe?" I repeat, perking up. "There's water nearby?"

He smiles at me, his eyes twinkling. "I woke up earlier than you, if you remember." I make a face. How could I forget? He chuckles before continuing. "While you were fast asleep, I found an opening in the back that leads to a small pool. One we can bathe in safely."

"Oh man—that sounds so good right now." I'm soaked in sweat and was already dreading trying to clean up as best as I could. "It's so hard to sleep when I feel dirty."

"You will not have to," he reassures me.

This might be the best gift anybody has ever given me. We decide we may as well bathe first so that we can eat and drink in comfort. Like a gentleman, Archion stays out while I venture through the narrow opening in a shadowed corner of the cave. No wonder I didn't notice it.

When I step through, there's light streaming in from a

crack, illuminating the gently rippling water. To call it a pool would be generous, but it is deep enough that I can get in halfway up my body, up to my waist.

I jump in with all of my clothes on, needing to rinse them out after everything they've been through. I don't linger though, cognizant of the fact that Archion is waiting for me. I wring out my clothes, lay them out to dry on a flat rock, and then wash myself briskly.

Some soap would be nice, but I just use some of the sand at the bottom instead. Exfoliation, right? Gotta make the best things. That's one lesson I've learned here on Tajss.

Feeling much better, I climb out and put on the damp but now cleaner clothes. Finger-combing my hair, I walk back out into the main cave.

Archion turns to me.

"Done?" he asks.

"Yes. Thank you."

He inclines his head, his eyes lingering on me.

"I will be out shortly," he murmurs, walking past me to enter the pool.

I turn towards the rations and start to nibble to distract myself from the fact that Archion—a very naked Archion—is bathing just a few feet away from me. I feel a rush of warmth at the thought, at imagining his naked body, water droplets sliding down his impressive chest... The pool just barely covering his hip bones, if that...

I shake my head at myself in frustration, but I obviously can't control my thoughts when it comes to Archion. A recurring nuisance.

At least Archion is as good as his word, coming back out with damp hair in maybe a quarter of the time that it took me. Though that just means now I can stare at him and fantasize instead of just using my imagination. Sometimes, there's just no winning.

He comes over, taking some of the food as well.

"How do you feel?" he asks, taking a bite.

"Kind of sore," I confess. "I haven't exercised like that in...honestly, maybe ever."

He smiles at that, his eyes twinkling with humor.

"I understand. From what I have gleaned, your time on the ship did not require it of you. It is reasonable that you would be soft if you did not need to defend yourselves from any predators."

I guess that's true.

"Yeah, there weren't any predators on the ship. At least of the beast variety, anyway. There were some not-great people on the ship, which is kind of inevitable with any sizable population. But we had security to deal with that, people we could go to for help." I shrug. "I guess I never thought about it." I scan his body, appreciating how it looks, but now also doubly appreciating the amount of effort it takes to look like that. "How about you? Have you always been like this?" I ask, curious.

Did he come out of the womb a badass?

"No," he murmurs, meeting my eyes. "In truth, you have endured nothing compared to my Zmaj brothers. In terms of the physical beating we all received. Our training is brutal. It forces one to dig into the depths and retrieve the power needed to surmount any obstacle that may present itself."

I nod, bracing my elbow on my knee and propping my head on it. I don't take offense. To be as good as he is, I would guess the training would be no joke.

"Sounds like they deliberately pushed you to the edge."

"Yes," he agrees, his eyes turning distant. Remembering. "It was not only to harden us physically, but also to toughen us mentally." He focuses on me once more, his eyes clearing. "Because of it, I now know I can deal with any situation that I find myself in."

"But you hated it at the time?" I prod.

Was he ever like me, cursing his trainer? He frowns, his eyes distant.

"I did not hate it. It was difficult, but it was also an honor to be trained by my teachers. I knew what I was learning was important. And I held on to that thought when things were difficult. It helped that I had my brothers with me, training alongside me. Commiseration with peers is very helpful when going through difficult times."

I nod as I listen, completely understanding. If I didn't have the other women with me during that time down in the tunnels with Annabel... Yeah. Being part of a group is really important, especially when things are hard.

"How many people were training with you?" I ask.

"More than a few," he answers vaguely. "The teachers were the best—it was difficult to be included in such training. The selection process was rigorous."

He switches gears after that, talking about the specific kind of exercises they were put through.

"After the first segment of training, each one of us who still remained was left out in the desert for a week, alone. With no water, no food, and no weapons. In areas known to be breeding grounds for both guster and zemlja."

I listen as he details the exercise, shocked at the lengths to which these supposedly wonderful trainers pushed their students.

"Did anybody ever get really hurt?" I ask, shaking my head. "That's real danger they put you in!"

"Yes," he says simply. "But the training is necessary. It culls out the weak."

Wow.

"If you say so," I murmur, not agreeing with that. What was the point of training if you were severely injured or worse? But I let it go because he clearly does not have the same perspective I do on the subject. "And you're still with the same people now?" I ask. "Is that who you live with?"

He pauses for a moment. Considering what to tell me?

"Yes. I still live with my brothers. The training was meant simply to weed out those who do not have the mental and physical fortitude needed, but it also forms a bond among those who remain..."

I listen to him, at the same time pondering the answers to the questions I've been asking.

It's clear he isn't giving me complete answers, or all the information. Not that that's a surprise, really. I know the Tribe Elders are suspicious specifically because he's such a closed book. I don't expect him to reveal everything to me so quickly.

Still... I trust him. It's not completely logical, but something in me tells me that I can, despite everything I don't know. Even if I don't consider his deliberately vague and short answers, it's clear there must be more going on than he's saying—especially when taking into account the supernatural experiences I've had around his arrival. I know that.

I'm also confident he'll tell me the rest in his own time. He has prior loyalties, something I have experience with myself, so I understand. I'm okay with waiting on the rest of the story.

Even if the Elders aren't.

## ARCHION

*I* find myself telling Nora more than I plan to, though still not as much as she is asking for. As much as I know she likely wants. It is different from keeping that same information from the Tribe Elders. I do not like keeping anything from her, but I must.

There is much more at stake than just my feelings on the matter. That's why I decide to get out of sight of her trusting eyes. I tell her am going to go hunt for meat. Some time away will hopefully settle these feelings, help me regain perspective.

I circle around the rock formation, searching out other caves, both smaller and larger. Fortunately it does not take me long to find one of the smaller creatures that dwells in caves.

The gretba hisses at me from behind its hiding place, its pale gray fur standing on end, large eyes glinting at me. It tries to run, but my lochaber is swift and accurate. It is dead before it knows what happened. It is not the largest prey, but it is round, with more than enough meat for both Nora and me.

I decide to skin and dress it before I bring it back. That will keep some of the blood away from where we are staying. Also, the creature could be seen as attractive to tender-hearted females such as Nora, round and furry as it is. I do not want her to feel badly about eating it.

When I return with the prepared animal, Nora brightens.

"Oh! You caught something!"

"Yes," I say with a smile. "I will start a fire and we will have a feast." I do not think I have ever felt more satisfied at having felled a creature for food. I stoke a small fire, carefully building it with some shelter from the wind outside. Once it is strong enough to sustain itself, I pull out my knife and cut pieces of meat to cook over the open flame.

"Smells delicious," Nora murmurs as she watches from next to me. "What kind of animal is it?"

"A gretba. One of the creatures that dwells in the caves," I explain. "Here—this piece is done."

I give her one of the small pieces, the outside now an attractive golden brown. Gretba have a high fat content and are known for seeking out salt deposits to lick. It should be good even without the advantage of seasonings.

"Careful—it is still hot."

She nods, tearing off a piece and letting it cool before popping it into her mouth. Her eyes widen as the flavor permeates her mouth.

"Oh my goodness, it's so good," she murmurs around her mouthful, closing her eyes.

I smile, feeling a deep sense of satisfaction at watching her eat what I have provided. She finishes that piece and I hand her a larger one.

"Thank you," she murmurs. "But you eat too. I think there's a bottomless pit inside me after all that working out," she mutters.

I nod, taking some meat for myself.

"You have worked hard today," I agree. "Eat until you are full."

She smiles at that, taking a healthy bite.

"I'm not going to argue against that."

I return the smile, biting into the tender morsel. The meat is good. Tender and flavorful. The smoke from the fire also helps. We are quiet then as we finish the meat I have cooked, leaving a bit left over for later. Much of the animal still remains to the side, uncooked.

"We should smoke the remainder of the meat before it attracts predators," I comment.

Nora nods, wiping her hands clean.

"All right. I can cut up the rest of it. How big do you want the pieces?" she asks.

"About this big and this long," I say, holding my hands out to measure. "If they are too big, they will take longer to smoke."

"Okay, got it."

She turns away, taking out her knife to break down the rest of the meat. Because she is doing that, I can work on a makeshift pit just outside our cave mouth to do the actual smoking. I gather rocks from around the cave to build a small well-like structure, finding a large flat one that I can use to mostly cover the top. It will not be perfect, but it will get the job done. I feed more fuel to the fire and turn back towards Nora to survey the cuts of meat that she has made so far.

"Can you cut them about half as thick?" I ask, noticing the sizes. "These will take too long to cook through."

She straightens, huffing out an irritated breath as she blows her hair out of her face. She looks over at me.

"I don't think that's necessary. They're pretty small already."

"They are small," I agree, keeping my own voice calm. "But

they should be smaller still."

Groaning, she shakes her head.

"You're kind of a control freak aren't you?" she mutters, hacking into the pieces a little too forcefully now. I wince. I hope she is not imagining they are me. I do not respond to the insult, not wanting to anger her further. When she picks up some pieces and brings them out to the makeshift smoker, I again have to correct her, this time over the manner in which she puts the cuts of meat inside.

"They cannot all be towards one section. An even layer is the best method. Usually, I like to start from the outside edge and work inward, with at least a finger width of space so they all have room."

"The rest of it is going to get filled up anyway," she responds sharply. "Why does it matter if we fill up one section first and then move on?"

She continues muttering to herself under her breath.

"I am sorry, but this is the traditional way to smoke game meat and has lasted hundreds of years, even past the Devastation. I do know what I am speaking of. If we do not do it in this manner, the quality of the resulting meat will not be as good."

I hold on to my patience without straining. I know her bickering is not really because she is disagreeing with me, or because she finds my comments truly angering. Her mood has plummeted because she is overtired from the grueling day. She is not accustomed to pushing herself this hard. I have seen this happen before with others. She has simply reached her limit.

"It's easier to do it this way," she continues, deliberately putting the meat down in the same pattern she was putting it in before. Standing her ground. It is clear that she needs to feel as though she is correct. I can give her that. Smoking the meat perfectly is not as important as her mental well-being.

"As you wish," I murmur softly, bowing slightly.

I take the opportunity to leave her to the task. I see a flash of consternation on her face, as if she feels regret that I am retreating, that she has insulted me enough to push me away. But I am not retreating because I am offended or angry. She is clearly overwhelmed, and I can see that. I think perhaps I can find something to help her mood.

"I am going to go scavenge for anything else I might find," I explain while I retreat to the mouth of the cave. "I will be back shortly."

I hope I can find her something that will appease her fire. Giving her time alone, time to calm, will also help.

So I go for a walk, staying near enough to the cave that I will hear Nora if she cries out for help. I also cannot venture too far in case the sandstorm picks up again. I stay near the grouping of rocks where the cavern is located, traveling around it and into various caves that have less protection from the elements, with holes in the ceilings and tunnels that lead into dark interiors. I do not explore too deeply as I walk, keeping my senses alert for any danger.

Fortunately the journey is trouble-free. And I find what I need when I least expect it. I walk between two boulders, planning the easiest path to another small opening I see, when a surprising and welcoming sight greets me—flowers.

A large patch of them, growing up from the rocky soil between the boulders, in a crevice that receives partial sunlight. Beautiful and rare, just like Nora. I step closer, scanning them carefully to ensure they are not a poisonous variety.

Each one is as big across as my hand, made up of five large petals with frilled edges in an overlapping, almost spiral pattern. The edges are a mixture of a bright yellow and a fiery orange, fading into a light green, a bright blue, and then a center that is a blood-red color, punctuated with a deeper orange, funnel-like center. Fihibs—one of the few flowers here on Tajss that aren't poisonous.

I crouch and carefully cut the stem of the prettiest one. I know Nora will enjoy it.

I turn to make my way back to the cave. It has been close to an hour by this point, enough time for her to have calmed. At least, that is my hope. The return is as trouble-free as the walk out.

When I step back into the cave, I smell the smoking meat and see Nora just stepping out from the crevice that leads to the pool, her washed clothes in her hands. When she sees me, she slows to a stop, her face turning wary.

It is clear she expects an unpleasant attitude to return with me, for me to be angry or irritated with her. Well, she is going to be disappointed.

I hold up the flower. "I brought something back for you," I say.

Her eyes go down to what I am holding. She blinks at it or a moment before her face clears in recognition with a growing excitement I was hoping for.

"Oh!" she exclaims softly, swiftly closing the distance between us. "It's gorgeous, Archion!"

She reaches out to take it, her eyes wide.

"Wait," I murmur before she can take it. She looks up at me questioningly. "Fihibs are known for more than their beauty."

"Give me your tongue."

"My tongue?" Nora asks, somewhat incredulous.

I nod once more. She bites her lip, her eyes meeting my own. Then, hesitantly, she opens her mouth.

With a finger, I reach into the funnel-like center of the fihib blossom and scoop out some of the thick, golden nectar in the interior. I put my finger into her waiting mouth, dripping the sweet nectar onto her tongue. Her eyes widen once more when she closes her mouth.

I suck off the rest of the nectar from the same finger, the sweetness coating my tongue. Her eyes darken as she sees me do so. I know something that would be even sweeter than the nectar. Stepping even closer, I grip her hip in my hand and bend down to set my mouth against Nora's soft pink lips.

She sighs against my mouth, and I use the opportunity to slide my tongue over hers, tasting her sweetness combined with the nectar. Delicious. My grip tightens on her hip. The feel of her soft mouth against mine, the taste of her... It is so much better than I dreamed.

She melts against me as the kiss continues, deepens, the front of her pressing up against my body. I can feel the softness of her breasts and stomach, the rapid beat of her heart. She makes a small sound of enjoyment, of surrender, at the back of her throat. A rush of heat has me tightening my hand on her even more.

Too hard! I immediately release her hip. And then know I do not have the self-control to keep going.

I break the kiss. I leave my mouth almost touching hers, and take a deep breath filled with her scent, the sweetness of it rivaling the flower's perfume. I want to taste her lips again. I want to be even closer. But I am weak. I do not have the discipline. I move back just enough so we are not pressed together.

"Let us not fight," I breathe into her ear.

She nods slowly, taking the flower as I release it, our fingers brushing. Even that fleet of a touch affects me.

"Okay," she whispers, her desire-filled eyes not leaving my own.

The air is heavy and hot between us with unfulfilled desire. My eyes drop to her lips once more despite myself. How will I survive any more time alone with her?

## 13

### NORA

*T*he meat still has some more time to smoke, but night has fallen. There's nothing more we can do right now, really.

If I thought it was difficult to be around Archion before, it's almost impossible now. That kiss... My lips tingle at just the thought of it. I really didn't see that coming. Not after how irritable I was.

I look over at Archion as I settle back down onto my pallet. I pick up the flower he brought, bring it up to my face, and take a deep breath of its sweet scent. That's a mistake. I feel a rush of heat. I don't think I'm ever going to be able to look at, touch, or taste a fihib again without thinking of Archion. Not that it's a bad thing.

I must have made some kind of noise because Archion looks over at me from where he is checking on the meat.

"Is something wrong?" he asks.

I shake my head, blushing at being caught mooning over a flower.

"No," I say, feeling ready to unravel at eye contact alone. How embarrassing.

His eyes travel down to my lips and linger there. My fingers tighten on the stem of the flower. At least I'm not the only one feeling this way. But he simply looks away again, ignoring the sexual tension that never really leaves us. The kiss just ramped things up.

It was such a surprise. I really expected him to come back and confront me about my terrible mood, knowing I deserved it. He came back with a gorgeous flower instead, and completely melted my heart—followed quickly by my panties with that scorching kiss. If that isn't a one-two punch, I don't know what is.

We've both been quiet ever since, retreating to our respective corners, both of us trying to ignore the tension. It's not working all that well, at least not for me. I don't think it's working for him either.

Maybe conversation will help divert our attention. I clear my throat, searching for a topic. Luckily, I have plenty of questions I haven't gotten answers to yet.

"Does the group you belong to have a name?" I venture. He might not answer, but at least it's something else to focus on. He looks over at me, raising a brow. I can almost feel his hesitation in revealing even just the name. Maybe he won't answer...

"The Order."

I nod, trying not to give away my surprise at the fact that he actually responded. I don't want him to clam back up. Maybe I can get more out of him.

"Are they anywhere near here?"

He shrugs.

"No." A pause as he turns around and walked towards his own pallet. "Is Tajss at all like your home planet?"

Turning it around on me, huh? I shrug. I don't have anything to hide.

"Honestly, I've never been to Earth. All I know about it

comes from the videos and books that we had on the ship. But, judging from that...it's completely different." I try to remember the images, the video. Honestly, I haven't really thought about Earth for a while now. It was never truly real to me anyway. "For one thing, most of Earth is made up of water. And though it has deserts, it also has variation. Lush forest, icy cold places, more temperate areas that are somewhere in the middle."

Archion nods, his gaze interested as he settles onto the pallet.

"Did you like the ship?" he asks next, cocking his head. "I cannot imagine never being outside."

I could see that.

"It was all I ever knew," I start slowly. "It was definitely more comfortable than Tajss is. And there was work to keep me busy along with hours and hours of media to go through if I was bored. Plenty of people." I shrug, thinking it over. "Yeah, I guess there are parts of it I definitely miss. But I also can't deny that I feel so much more alive here on Tajss. Life is just more...immediate, I guess. There isn't as much room for anxiety—not that I don't find pockets to have attacks anyway," I add with a grimace. "And being outside is nice, even in this ridiculous heat."

He smiles at that.

"Also, the bathing."

I grin.

"Yes, being able to bathe in water here is great. It almost makes the sweating worth it." I watch his face, enjoying the way his eyes crinkle at the corners when he grins. But, let's be honest here—everything he does is sexy to me. "What about you? How does the Tribe compare to the Order? Do you miss it?"

He doesn't answer this time, going silent instead. After a few beats, he speaks quietly.

"You are digging," he observes, meeting my eyes, his own watchful.

"Am I?" I ask, holding his gaze steadily.

I'm not going to take the question back. He looks away, seemingly put off. It's like there's some tether keeping him from treading onto that specific conversational ground. The more I speak to him, the more sure I am that he's sworn some kind of oath, made some kind of promise involving secrecy. He's silent for another few beats. But when he speaks again, he doesn't try to justify or explain it away. He just turns the direction of the conversation to the Elders.

"How do you feel?" he asks, turning to meet my eyes once more. "How do you like the Tribe? What do you think of the Elders?"

It isn't a normal question, or at least it doesn't feel like it. It's almost like...he's looking at this conversation like it's a chess match, or some other similar game of strategy. Fighting my question with a question that is difficult for me. I can't speak against the Elders, not with the hospitality they've afforded me and my friends. It just isn't right.

As I stare back at Archion in silence, I start to wonder if I'll ever truly get to know him. Is his loyalty to this Order too deep? How far does this shield, his oath, or whatever this wall he's erected between us reach? And if it really is that deep, that intense, then what's the point in growing more attached to him.

Like I'm afraid I will. I can feel it happening already. Is he always going to keep me at arm's length around certain topics?

For the first time, I start to wonder if I've read this whole situation wrong. Maybe I'm not supposed to be with Archion. Maybe the visions were saying something else entirely. I don't know anymore.

I stand up and say, "I'm gonna take a bath," and I turn towards the opening.

"Very well," he returns, his voice just as reserved as my own. It doesn't make me feel any better.

As soon as I step into the small cavern with the spring, I hear him get up and start to train in the now-empty main cavern. The distinct sound of shadow sparring is clear, and I know if I look out I'll see him jumping and punching and kicking, swinging his lochaber at opponents only he can see. He's always taking the opportunity to hone skills that are already razor sharp. Maybe he's also using it as a way to get out some frustration. I guess it doesn't matter.

I slide out of my clothes and step into the warm water, sighing as it laps against my skin. I move over to the side, lie back, and let my legs float. I'm just drifting, trying to empty my mind of everything. It doesn't work all that great. I keep going over everything I know despite myself. The visions, the dreams. Archion's character, which obviously veers towards heroic. And then everything I don't know, which is basically anything about his past. I know he is a part of this Order, but I don't know anything about the group. Or what he was really doing in the desert that day he stumbled on us. I don't think he's lying, but I also don't think that being honest and open is his priority right now.

Adding the attraction between us to all of that, along with the suspicion the Elders clearly have about him... Yeah. This is a mess. A conclusion that I'd already come to.

I sigh, letting my eyes fall closed. I keep fighting myself, but no matter how much I try to relax, I just can't. Until, finally admitting defeat, I pull myself out of the pool and dry off. I can still hear Archion moving around out there so I know he's not asleep yet.

I dress quickly and walk back out into the main cave and

to my pallet. He looks over at me but then turns back towards the entrance of the cave.

"Aren't you going to sleep?" I ask, pulling the covers over me. I yawn, the day finally catching up with me despite my worries.

"I will guard us," Archion murmurs. "Sleep well, Nora."

"Okay," I murmur, my eyes already closing. "Don't stay up all night," I say, but I don't know if he listens. I'm out like a light. Unfortunately, it doesn't last. Is this going to become a pattern?

"Nora!" My eyes snap open at my name.

"What?"

"Nora, wake up!"

The urgency in Archion's voice has me sitting up and looking over towards him in alarm. Then I actually register those weird tapping sounds that my subconscious heard but couldn't decipher. What is that?

Only then do I understand what I'm seeing, my brain finally coming fully online. The darkness outside now has eyes and legs, and Archion is fighting it.

My mouth falls open as I stare.

Are those...giant spiders?

Maybe four of them are trying to attack Archion at once. About waist high and maybe as big as large dogs, their bodies are black with gray striations, which is probably why I didn't see them right away.

Six thin, insect-like legs on each side of their massive, segmented bodies scramble for purchase as they fight. To make matters worse, the backs of their bodies don't end in points like spiders' bodies do.

Rather, they have an oddly curved tail with a sharp end that curves over their backs, almost like a short scorpion tail. One of them tries to stab Archion as I watch.

His lochaber chops off the knife-sharp end in a quick

slice. The creature steps back, baring its sharp teeth. I expect some kind of sound to come out, but it doesn't.

To make it even more disorienting, its face doesn't look like quite like an insect's. It has only two eyes in an elongated face, ending in lipless mouth with sharp teeth. From the top of its head grow pointed ears and long, almost ram-like horns that curve back.

What the hell are they? Spider-goat-scorpions?

They're crowding around Archion, but he's holding them back with his fighting prowess, the lochaber swinging and stabbing while he shifts out of the way of attacks, leaps over some, kills one with a harsh stab to the head.

Then I see a slightly smaller one has pushed through an opening in Archion's guard.

It comes straight towards me—that lights a fire under me.

"Shit!" I mutter, scrambling out of my pallet and reaching for the electro-stick right next to me.

It runs fast, its thin legs propelling that improbably fat body towards me faster than I would've expected. It opens its mouth, displaying those sharp teeth, longer fangs directly in the front dripping glistening saliva.

Now that it's closer, I see that the bottom third of its legs is covered in a dark, rough looking fur, and its eyes are a deep purple.

"Oh my God," I mutter to myself, my feet gripping the ground as I hold the stick in front of me. It's shaking. Probably because I'm fully shaking with fear at this point.

This is so not like training!

In fact, all of that training goes right out the window as that thing rushes at me. All the technique, all of the ways to block, how to move my feet. I don't remember any of it.

Screaming, I stab the creature with the end of the stick, hoping against hope that it has enough juice. I aim for the mouth as it rushes towards me. It knocks me back onto the pallet.

I scream, but I keep the stick pressed up against its mouth as its body covers me, caging me in with its legs.

Come on! The stick finally ignites with a bright blue flash, all of that burning electricity hitting the creature at once.

It freezes on top of me. Is it working? It begins to jerk and convulse. I scramble backwards, out from under it, keeping the stick up against its face. It continues to jerk, smoke coming out from its body as it is electrocuted. I smell burning hair. Ewwww. And then it falls to the ground.

I take three quick steps back out of range as soon as it does. I'm breathing hard, my gaze fixed on the creature.

It jerks on the ground, attempting to regain its feet. It isn't dead, just stunned.

Should I step closer? Try to shock it again? Or will I just be putting myself in more danger if I do that?

I risk a glance over at Archion, only to find him surrounded by three carcasses. His lochaber swings and lops off three of the still-standing creature's legs. It falls to the ground, attempting to scramble away now. Archion puts it out of its misery with one swift stab to the head.

Not waiting to make sure it is indeed dead, he turns towards me and leaps across the cavern.

The one I stunned is still attempting to get up when Archion stabs it in the back of the head too, the crunch of the blow nauseating.

I stare down at the now-still creature, my mouth agape in shock. I swallow, slowly lowering the electro-stick. He's handled the whole group of them with an efficiency that's truly humbling.

"Are you hurt?"

I tear my gaze away from the dead creature in front of me

and look up to Archion's face. He scans me intently before meeting my eyes.

"Nora—are you hurt?" he asks again.

I shake my head dumbly.

He nods sharply, turning to look back over at the cave entrance. Bodies litter the area directly outside and inside. A large pile of meat directly in front of our sanctuary. Like a warning to any other beasts that would even consider breaching the safe space Archion has found for us.

I shiver, hugging myself.

# 14

## NORA

*A*rchion spends time dragging the carcasses out of the cave before settling down at the cave entrance again. Breescha. That's what those horrifying spider monsters are called, apparently.

Archion is obviously wide-awake now and not in any mood to sleep, but he tells me to lie down.

"Rest," he urges. "I will keep watch."

I nod. There isn't anything else to do.

I settle down in my pallet, unsure about if I'll be able to get even a moment's rest that night. But eventually my heart settles down and sleep starts to knock on my door again—a welcome surprise.

My eyes stay on Archion, his distinctively protective stance at the cave entrance the last thing I see before I fall asleep and dream of him. Not in a vision way, in a purely fantasizing way.

He is the perfect hunter-warrior, as male as one can be. Mysterious, bold, and deadly. He makes my knees go soft. Even my dream—it's fuzzy, just a jumble of images, of his face, his eyes.

His body.

There's a strange juxtaposition to our attraction. The silent glances and heavy tension colliding with the softness of the flower he brought back to me. And the harshness with which he protected me.

When I wake up the next morning, he's still on my mind. As the days have gone by, there's no denying the attraction between us. After being alone in this cave with him... Honestly, I can barely muster up the restraint needed to keep my clothes on around him.

As if on cue, he emerges from the narrow opening on the heels of that thought, obviously fresh from the spring. I can't look away. He's gloriously, perfectly naked. Completely comfortable in his own skin. And why wouldn't he be?

Tall, with that frame heavy with muscle, his smooth, tan skin almost glows with health. I see his back muscles flex as he stretches his wings out a little, the curve of his ass and the muscle of his thighs catching my eyes.

I swallow, feeling my mouth water in response. I should look away. Really I should. Any moment now... I'm only human, damn it! Once he's covered up again, I look away just in time to avoid him catching me ogling him.

"Good morning," he says, his eyes scanning my face. As if he wasn't just naked in front of me. "Are you hungry?"

I nod, standing up. I know my cheeks are pink, but I blush so much around him at this point I'm hoping he might think my cheeks just redden randomly or something. Hey, I need to hold on to my illusions where I can.

"I'm just going to clean up real fast," I say, looking away. I hurry over to the spring myself, trying to pretend I'm not running away.

I have to just accept the fact that I'm going to be flushed around him ninety percent of the time. There's just no way around it. It doesn't take too long to get myself back together. I splash water on my face and give myself a firm pep talk. I'm a grown woman. I can do this.

When I come back out, Archion is already laying out the thinly cut meat he managed to smoke to perfection. Despite my own stubbornness. Thinking back, I have no idea why I argued against him about it. He obviously has a lot more experience with smoking game meat than I do.

When I look at the food he's put out, I see something new —a small bowl of deep red berries.

"Oh, it looks great!" I remark as I settle down beside the food. I pick up the bowl with the berries bringing it closer so I can have a look. "What are these?"

"Xara berries," he says, a tinge of adorable excitement in his voice. "I gathered them early this morning before you woke up. Try them—they are delicious."

He doesn't have to tell me twice. I take a few of the smooth, round morsels. The skin is taut, the berries plump with juice. I pop one into my mouth and bite down.

"Mmm," I hum, my eyes automatically closing as it bursts, releasing sweet juice reminiscent of the nectar from the flower he brought me yesterday. And, just like that, my thoughts return to the kiss that followed. And...there's the blush. What a surprise.

I open my eyes to tell him they're good, but when I meet his hot gaze, I have to avert my own.

"They're really good," I murmur, popping more into my mouth. "Thank you."

"Of course," he murmurs. "Here, have some meat."

I nod, taking the piece he offers and bringing it to my mouth right away too. Maybe if I keep my mouth full, I won't have to talk. Anything to avoid awkward conversation right then. Luckily, he doesn't push for more.

We eat breakfast in a calm silence that I can really appreciate. I end up breaking the quiet myself when he stands up.

"Where you going?" I ask as he steps towards the exit.

"I am going to go find the cart. Stay here. I won't be long."

The confidence in his voice eases the panic that wants to rise in my gut. I am so not equipped to be alone here on Tajss, but I trust that he wouldn't leave me here if he didn't think it was safe.

"Be careful," I call out after him.

He turns back to me, his gaze serious.

"I will."

I watch as he heads off, every cell in my body vibrating with need. Anxiety and attraction is an interesting mixture. Okay, I need to distract myself, or I might very well go crazy.

First I tidy up the minimal mess we've made. Then I go back to the spring to take a full bath and wash the clothes I wore yesterday. Then I put on the clean ones that are dry.

That done, I run through the moves that Archion has shown me so far, remembering how I froze the night before. I need to practice so the moves become second nature, so I don't have to think when there's a fight. Hopefully, if I practice enough, the moves will come naturally.

Despite my best efforts to keep my mind off of how much time has passed since Archion left, I still find myself sitting down on my pallet and waiting for him towards the end. With nothing else to do, I start to flip through the notebook Penelope gave me. That's what he finds me doing when he finally returns around midday.

I quickly tuck the book away and get up to help him load the smoked meat into the cart. I know he noticed the book, but he doesn't comment as we work side by side. It's not like he doesn't have a billion secrets of his own.

"Do you think we can leave for the Tribe today?" I ask as we load the last of the meat.

"I believe so," Archion says, looking outside. "The winds have died down—"

The distinctive sound of a meteorite hitting the ground interrupts his statement. The first is followed quickly by more of the same. When I look outside, the sand outside the cave being bombarded by meteors. We watch in silence for a moment, nonplussed.

"However...perhaps we should wait a bit longer before returning back to your home," Archion says.

I snort out a laugh, shaking my head. "Yeah. That's probably a good idea."

So there we are, once again. Alone in the cavern. Well, not counting the elephant in the room, our attraction, hanging out with us.

Archion grins at me, grabs his pack, and rummages around in it.

"What are you looking for?" I ask, curious.

He winks at me as he produces a flask I haven't seen before. A wine flask.

"To help us pass the time," he says, passing it over to me.

I raise a brow at him. "You're full of surprises," I say.

His eyes darken. "You have no idea," he returns huskily.

Excited and unnerved by the comment—while also being reminded of the wall of secrets that remains between us—I tip the wine flask to my mouth and take a healthy gulp. It burns down my throat. I give a small, sputtering cough, patting my chest.

He takes the flask when I hand it back over to him, his gaze filled with admiration that I don't think the act warrants. He shakes the flask, checking the level of liquid left in it.

"Not so soft as one would think," he murmurs, his eyes tracing my face. And then my body.

I shiver, as his gaze traces lines of heat wherever it lands. I'm not ready to face that yet. In an effort to break the rising sexual tension, I call upon my inner nerd. A game never hurts any situation, right?

Crouching on the cave floor, I use my finger to draw a tic-tac-toe hash mark in the dirt.

"Do you want to play a game?" I ask, looking up at him.

He nods, his gaze already on the impromptu mark.

"Yes. How do we play?"

He crouches down across from me.

"Well, we each pick our symbol and..."

I show him how to play. And, unsurprisingly, he picks it up immediately.

"Ah," he says. "I understand. Would you like to go first?"

Always the gentleman.

"Sure." I start and we take turns until I make a row on the diagonal.

"Good game," he praises me. "Again." He wins the next one. And the next one.

Catching on to his tricks, I concentrate and fight back until we're basically evenly matched, our wins and losses averaging out to fifty-fifty. More importantly, the game succeeds in returning us to neutral ground before things go too far.

And, luckily, we don't have to while away a whole lot more time before the meteorite shower is over. Within a few hours, Archion goes out and gives us the all clear.

Taking the cart, he pushes it out, guiding us towards where the flaming rocks have hit the sand.

We already loaded the meat into the compartment for the food, but the main compartment of the car is still open and ready to take the meteors and the glass that we find.

"Stay in sight," Archion orders.

I nod. I have no desire to be separated from him out here. We work quickly, gathering everything that will fit in the cart. I'm not sure if the glass is any different, or if any of the rocks we are able to gather are unique either. But that isn't for us to discern anyway, so I don't worry about it. By the time the cart is almost full, there isn't anything left to collect.

"Let us try over this next dune," Archion suggests.

I nod, wiping the sweat off my brow as we continue our arduous hike over the sand. Unfortunately, that's when the wind decides to grow rough once more. Can't we catch a break? This trip really isn't raising my opinion of the desert.

"Let us take cover over there!" Archion calls out, trying to be heard over the wind.

I look over to where he gestures. It's another ridge, rock curved over the top of it, with a dune on each side to buffer it. It's deep enough that it will give us more than adequate coverage. It also has the added bonus of being close enough that we don't have to abandon the cart this time. Archion pushes forward as I trudge alongside him.

We make it in plenty of time before the sandstorm is anywhere near as severe as it was before. Setting the cart to cover the entrance in order to provide more cover, Archion turns towards me. Once again, we're alone in an enclosed space. Without anything to do. Archion's eyes meet mine, the knowledge of the situation clear in them. This time, there's nothing to be done about it. A sense of inevitability.

We've put it off and put it off so many times that the magnetic pull between us is like a living thing, a creature that started off easy to control, but now grown so wild and strong that it's irresistible. And how much do I really want to resist?

I give up. I want it, want him, too badly to keep denying myself. Even as I think of surrender, I feel the heat intensify inside me.

My skin tingles. I can feel my nipples tighten, the heat gathering low in my belly. It's like I've finally given my body permission to feel this real desire.

As he seems to with most things, Archion senses the shift in the air.

"Nora," he murmurs, closing the distance between us in two long strides. He doesn't wait to pull me close, wrapping his arms firmly around my waist. His eyes search my own, so close that the edges of his face are blurred.

I slide my hands up his chest to wrap around his neck.

That's the only signal he needs. He closes the distance between our mouths, claiming mine wantonly. The kiss is hot, deep, saturated with the desire we've both been holding back for too long.

Oh, God.

That kiss before had been... But this... Maybe it's because I know we're not going to stop at just a kiss this time.

His hands slide down my back, down to my butt, gripping and squeezing. I press closer against him, going up on my toes as I feel the hard evidence of his arousal against my belly. I deliberately rub against it, feeling completely out of control. He groans at the friction, breaking the kiss to start stripping me out of my clothes.

"I want to touch your skin," he mutters, moving quickly despite his gentle touch. Just like with everything else, he's amazingly good at getting my clothes off without any awkwardness, until I'm down to a bra and panties in front of him.

He stops then, his eyes intent as he traces me with his gaze, lingering on my breasts, my hips, but taking all of me in.

"You are so beautiful," he says hoarsely, reaching up with one hand to cup the soft curve of my breast.

My breath shudders out of me as his thumb moves to rub against my hardened nipple, poking out against the cup.

He looks up at the sound. "Good?" he asks, stopping the small movement.

I nod, biting my lip. "Yes," I sigh. "Very good."

He watches my face this time when he continues, his thumb rubbing deliberately.

My eyes half close, my lips part slightly. The touch is so small, but it's Archion touching me. And because of that, it feels like so much more.

His hand slowly slides up to my shoulder, hooking the strap of my bra. Then his other hand slides to the other strap.

His eyes drop from my face to watch as he pulls the bra down, sliding the straps down my shoulders and arms. The cups go down with it, leaving my bra wrapped around my waist. Leaving my breasts exposed.

I take a shuddering breath, watching his eyes as his hands move down to cup the soft weight of them. His eyes are wondering as he moves his thumbs, rubbing the hardened tips, watching his hands touch me.

A sharp, tingling sensation flows through me at the light touch. At the look in his eyes, the naked want.

"You are so soft," he murmurs, squeezing me gently.

I sigh, sliding my hands up and down his upper arms, my eyes half closing at the slow, sensual touch.

"You should take your clothes off too," I suggest, watching him.

He nods, but instead of moving to touch his own clothes, he slowly drops to his knees in front of me, his eyes rising to my face.

"First you," he says, his fingers sliding around the thin sides of my panties, wrapped around my hips.

I swallow as they linger there.

His eyes are dark as they hold mine, the question in them clear. He's waiting for me to say yes. Waiting for me to agree we should go down this path.

Is it smart? He's an outsider, something the Tribe Elders have made quite clear. Even apart from their suspicion of him and his intentions, he hasn't been open and honest about his background with me. So much can go wrong here. But I don't even know why I'm thinking of any of this.

My answer is almost a foregone conclusion. I feel like this has been barreling towards us ever since Zoe transmitted that vision to me. I want him too badly to stop myself for all the practical reasons.

"Yes," I breathe, cupping the side of his handsome face. "Yes, Archion."

His eyes blaze even hotter as he leans forward to press his lips gently against the soft skin of my exposed belly. But he doesn't pull my panties down right away.

He undoes the hooks of my bra strap and pulls it away from my body, his hands gentle and quick. He buries his face against my midsection for a moment, his big hands smoothing around my body to cup my butt, squeezing, kneading hard. My hands slide into his silky hair, the firm touch exactly what I wanted, the tight embrace helping me relax a little. I don't know if that's why he suddenly slowed down, if he felt my nerves. But I appreciate it either way.

After a few moments of that warm, needy embrace, his hands slide into the sides of my underwear again. And this time, there's no teasing.

He leans back so he can skim them down my hips, down my thighs. I lift one foot and then other, stepping out of the small scrap of fabric. Completely exposed now. Completely vulnerable to whatever Archion wants to do.

I shiver slightly as that realization hits me, an edge of trepidation hitting me on the heels of a wave of lust at that knowledge. It only makes everything seem even more intense.

The feeling of the air flowing over my naked skin, the weight of Archion's eyes as they look me over, the feel of his fingertips sliding up and down my thighs, the light touch spreading goosebumps over me.

He leans forward and kisses the front of me, his breath hot against my most sensitive parts.

"I want to kiss you here," he growls, his fingers sliding between my legs from behind, finding my folds wet and hot with my need for him.

I gasp, arching forward towards him, not expecting the touch. Growling, he lifts one of my thighs and places it over his shoulder, pressing his face against that most delicate and intimate part of me.

"Oh!"

I grip him tight, trying to get my balance on one foot as his tongue comes out to lick at me, curious and not at all hesitant. Oh God!

Then he discovers my clitoris. My eyes almost cross, my body swaying as he hits it with the flat of his tongue.

And he's no dummy. He pauses for a moment as if assessing my reaction. Then he does it again, but this time much more focused on that spot. My toes curl as I thrust against him, unable to control the motion of my hips.

It feels too damn good. So much better than my own fingers. Is this what I've been missing all this time? This was why all those women would leave men's quarters on the ship with secret smiles. And here I was, wasting my time hanging out in the background.

Archion's hands grip my hips, holding me in place as he pushes in even deeper, his tongue moving faster against me. Hard, fast, and focused, the sensation is too much for me. Too much after all of the time spent avoiding the physical. Too much after all this flirting with Archion, all of this build up.

I fly apart.

Completely and utterly.

Crying out, I shove myself against him, my leg collapsing underneath me as the pleasure flows through me in an almost harsh wave. But Archion holds me up easily, moaning against me as he continues to lick, to suck, to hold me up at that peak of pleasure as long as he possibly can, until I'm bent over him, my breath coming in gasps, my body limp with satiation. He kisses me softly before lifting his head away.

His hands are gentle as he positions me over one solid shoulder, his body shifting as he reaches for something. I'm soaking too deep in the glow of the orgasm I just had to wonder too hard about what he's doing. It's clear enough within a few seconds, anyway, when he tips me over carefully, directly onto our combined pallets, the unexpected softness of it on my back making me sigh and stretch in response.

I open my eyes as I feel Archion settle down between my legs again.

"Archion...?"

He lifts and spreads my legs, his eyes watching my face.

"You are small," he murmurs, sliding his fingers through my utterly saturated folds to circle my entrance.

I know my face is beet red now. There's something so much more intimate about eye contact while he touches me like that. He pushes a finger in, carefully.

My body slowly stretches to accommodate even that one thick finger. Still watching me, he leans down to lick at me, that finger still inside me. I relax a little, taking a deep breath.

I feel like I'm barreling through a whole lot of firsts right now.

When my body starts to move under him, that pleasure rises again where I didn't think it could, he starts to move that finger inside me, his tongue a delicious counterpoint to the small thrusts.

Then he tries to add another finger, and I flinch. He notices, of course.

He stops, raising his head.

"Are all human females this small?" he asks, his forefinger still inside me. He frowns. "Perhaps you are too small for me."

I swallow, rising up on my elbows once more so I can see him better. I need to tell him. I don't know why it makes me nervous, but it does.

"Uh...I guess we're smaller than Zmaj females probably were. But...I'm probably extra tight because..."

I bite my lip, my face so hot I'm surprised I don't just go up in flames.

"Because?" he prompts, his gaze intent on my face.

He's rubbing at my clit again with his thumb. It's not exactly helping me focus. I look away, unable to meet his eyes just then. Why does this feel more revealing then lying spread naked underneath him? I don't know why, but damn if it doesn't!

"Because...I've never been with anyone before," I get out in a rush.

His fingers still again.

"You have not...done this with anyone before?" he repeats.

I nod, still not looking at him. This is so embarrassing—

"Good," he growls.

That snaps my eyes back over to him.

"What?" I ask, gulping.

"Good," he repeats, leaning down to give me a quick, firm lick that makes me jump, startled. "I want your only memory to be of me."

His golden eyes are hot as closes his mouth over me and starts to suck. Oh... I fall back onto the pallet, my legs starting to move of their own accord. The pressure, the suction... It feels...

I clench my eyes shut, my hands gripping at the pallet on

either side of me.

Archion adds another finger, and there is stretch and pressure from it, but what he's doing with his mouth feels too good for it to distract me much. I feel the pleasure building once more, feel that heat gathering in my middle...

"Archion!" I cry out, my entire body arching as it hits me like a freight train, somehow different than the one before.

Making a low sound, he holds me down with a forearm across my hips, his eyes watching me as I shove myself against him. He keeps up that mind-blowing suction until I'm trying to pull away, until I tap out from the sensations. He kisses my inner thigh, his lips shiny from what he's been doing.

I take a few deep breaths, feeling...tingly.

I crack my eyes open again, taking in Archion's flushed and reddened face, the quick rise and fall of his chest, the clenched fists he's supporting himself on.

"Archion..." I sit up, feeling almost boneless. He stills as I cup the side of his face, leaning in to kiss him softly. "I...want you inside me."

He tenses against me.

"Yes," he agrees hoarsely.

Then he lays a kiss on me that leaves me breathless. All of that power, all of that desire, that need—directed at me. I've never felt so completely wanted. I break the kiss, both of us breathing harder.

"Take off your clothes," I order.

He pulls back, his eyes scanning my naked body as he undresses in much less time and with a fraction of the care he took with me.

He's utterly, wonderfully naked. I stare, taking in his muscled chest, his cobble stone abs, the thickly muscled thighs—and the truly awe-inspiring erection between them. My mouth goes dry and I try to swallow. I rest one of my hands against his chest, feeling the quickness of his heart-beats, and take him in my hand. He hisses, stiffening against me as I explore the thick length of him.

With so many Zmaj and human couples, word gets around about what they're working with. But being confronted with a penis this big... I swallow again, my curiosity sending my fingers to feel the ridges along the top of it, the biggest one at the base. All probably there for the female.

"Nora..." he groans as I swipe my thumb over the wetness at the head.

"Do you...do you have two?" I ask, wanting to get that out of the way. Two is...I mean one is a lot.

"Yes," he confirms, the small thrusts into my hand stopping. "Once my first is spent, the other will reveal itself from underneath my tail." A pause. "Is this...a problem?"

Startled, I look back up at him.

"A problem? No." I shake my head, kissing his cheek. "No. I just...you're very big."

Way to state the obvious.

"I will be careful," he reassures me, lowering me back down onto the pallet.

He layers his body over my own, his cooler skin pressing against mine, hot and sweaty from the heat and the orgasms I've already had.

I hum, wrapping my arms around his strong neck as he kisses me, enjoying the feeling of his larger, harder body above mine. Of his hardness pressing against the softness of my belly.

His hand slides down, stopping to cup my breast, but then moving on. It goes past my hip and to my thigh, lifting it and wrapping it around his hip so he can settle himself against me, his length sliding through my folds. We both gasp at that sensation.

Breaking the kiss, Archion rises up to his arms, his glaze taking in my no-doubt messy hair, my flushed face, my breasts, the curve of my waist, down to where his body is pressed up against my own.

His eyes take the same path back up to my face, his hips rotating against me, rubbing himself against me. Taking himself in hand, he notches the head against me.

"I will go slow," he murmurs, smoothing a hand down my side.

I nod, but I feel myself tense up a bit. There's a lot of him that has to fit inside me.

But he does go slow. And I've already had two orgasms to help me relax.

Still, it takes some effort. Archion comes down onto his elbows to kiss me, one of his hands reaching between us to start working on me as he continues the small in-and-out thrusts to make room for himself. It's a little uncomfortable, but it also feels good. He feels good above me.

After sliding my hands down his sides, I grip his ass, enjoying the feel of the taut muscle in my hands. Every part of him is so much harder than me, so much bigger.

I raise my other leg, so I can wrap them around his waist, pushing back against his next thrust. I cry out as he slides the rest of the way into me, his hips meeting mine, flush against each other.

Archion stops, breaking the kiss to suck in a deep breath. I can feel his pulse inside me. Can feel him throbbing.

We stay like that for a few moments, Archion's face so close to mine that all I can see is the gold of his eyes. It takes a second, but I start to relax around him a bit.

I feel impossibly full, but slowly, the discomfort that comes with it starts to abate. Archion must feel me relax somewhat under him because he leans down to kiss me gently.

"Good?" he asks, nuzzling the side of my face.

I nod, gripping his shoulders.

"Move, Archion," I murmur, wanting to feel the rest. I grind against him a little experimentally. Oh. That feels nice.

Archion isn't one to avoid a direction like that. Propping himself up on his forearms, he starts to move out in tiny increments and then back in even more slowly.

He tilts his head to look between us, to watch his length disappear into me once more. The sight is mesmerizing, even to me. Coupled with the feel of him pushing into me, the feel of him surrounding me... And the feel of those delicious ridges rubbing me in exactly the right way... I shudder as he bottoms out again, that last ridge at the very end pressing against me perfectly.

Before I know it, Archion is pumping into me with more speed, and I'm meeting him thrust for thrust, grinding against him on each downswing. My nails dig into his shoulders, my head kicking back as I feel that orgasm building once more. It feels different this time, a slower build. Maybe a deeper one. He starts to push into me harder, rubbing against me where I...

My body locks, the pleasure hitting me harder than expected, faster than I thought it would. I wrap my arms around him, tightening my legs, holding him as close as I can while the orgasm runs through me, while I clench down on him inside me.

I hear Archion make a sound above me, and then he shoves himself that last half inch back inside me, his erection jerking hard inside me as he joins me, his large body trembling. His head hangs down, his hair obscuring his face as we both start to come back down.

I feel like I've run a marathon. Every inch of me feels spent, like I'll just fall over if I try to get up.

Archion stirs above me, pulling out of me carefully and

rolling to the side. I immediately feel exposed and cold, though it's still as warm as ever, but then he wraps an arm around me and pulls me in securely against his side. I sigh, snuggling into him, settling my hand against his chest.

But my palm rubs against rougher skin on the side of his chest, where his arm usually covers it. It's a small spot, maybe a half an inch around.

Curious, I sit up, still fully ensconced in the afterglow, but the sight of his skin has me pausing. There's a scarred area there, a symbol carved into his skin, a lighter color than his normally tanned self. And its familiar.

I frown at it, my finger tracing it. It looks like a symbol Zoe revealed to me during that initial vision she gave me. One I didn't really focus on, there and gone as it was. It's two lines crossing each other in an X shape, but the top left and bottom right are extended out... Like two lochabers maybe?

Archion catches my hand gently and firmly moves it away from that symbol.

"You weren't supposed to have seen that."

I shake my head, looking up at his serious eyes. "What? Why? What is it?"

But he doesn't answer my questions. Rolling towards me, he raises my leg over his hip, nudging against me with his second erection.

His mouth covers my own, swallowing my murmur of surprise as he starts to sink into me again. I'm already sensitized from before, the inward glide of him firing all sorts of nerve endings. I shudder against him. It almost feels like I'm already close...

All of my questions fade away under his touch as he starts to push in and then out of me, slowly and carefully, our lips clinging together.

It's slower, lazier. But it feels...

It feels so good I can't think of anything else. So I don't.

## 15

## ARCHION

*F*inally, there is no sandstorm and no meteorite shower, and we can begin traveling back to the Tribe. I find myself reluctant to do so, and not just because I will have to face the Tribe Elders' suspicious faces. That is secondary. This time spent alone with Nora—I would not trade it for anything.

I look over at her as I push the cart. The suns shine down on her beautiful, glowing face, on her shining hair. I have a flash of an image, a picture of how she looked underneath me, pleasure suffusing her features, her skin gleaming with heat...

I force myself to look away, feeling that desire rise once more. Now that I have had a taste, I know I cannot stay away. It is a truth that I accept. Even my trainers always said to accept reality and work forward from that point.

"Archion?"

Nora's low voice brings me out of my thoughts.

"Yes?"

She steps closer to me, frowning.

"Did you hear that?"

I'm immediately alert, scanning the area, straining to hear. There. Had I not been so deep in my own thoughts, I would not have missed the slight sound. I will not allow that to happen again.

"Wait here," I order.

She nods, stopping next to the cart.

I carefully make my way up the next dune and then the next.

My quarry is not far at all, and that knowledge sends a chill down my spine. I need to be more aware of my surroundings, especially when I have Nora with me. She is depending upon me to protect her.

I clench my jaw as I look out at another invader camp. This one does not have nearly as many people as the first one I came across did. Ten total. Hmm. I watch them for a moment, almost immediately discarding my first thought which is to take a detour around them.

I do not want to put Nora at risk with a fight, but neither do I want to leave them alive. There is no telling in which direction they intend to go, and with Nora and the cart with me, slowing down any actions, the outcome of circling around them is highly uncertain.

Better to take care of the threat now.

I watch to ensure they are not going to be moving any time soon. When I am reasonably sure they plan to stay for some time, I carefully back away, staying low to the ground.

Then I do a circuit around their camp, scanning the ground as I do. I am looking for something very specific, something I vaguely remember should be in this area. I finally find it a bit of a distance away from their encampment —an oasis with a small spring and scraggly trees surrounding it.

I immediately start to circle the area, looking for that distinctive shift in the color of the sand. Sometimes, water bubbles up and mixes with the sand, not creating a pool of water, but rather a pit of almost liquid sand that is quite dangerous. If my memory serves me correctly, this oasis used to have one such pit that was quite surprisingly wide considering how small the actual spring is...

There.

An area where the sand is too smooth, the color just slightly off. I crouch down, not too close, reaching out and dipping my finger in. It comes away wet, sand sticking to it. Perfect.

I make my way back to Nora, where she is still waiting patiently next to the cart.

"There are invaders nearby," I explain in a low voice. "I am going to hide you here and lure them away."

Nora frowns, shaking her head.

"Wait, what? Lure them away? Why?"

"I do not want to leave them here, a danger that could stumble upon us at any time," I explain. "Better to take care of them now, while we know where they are. The group is small enough that I think I can do so."

She shakes her head, still not accepting my plan.

"How? How many is a small group?"

"About ten."

"Ten?" she asks, stepping closer. "How are you going to take on ten?"

I shake my head.

"I am not going to fight ten," I explain. "There is a sandpit I found not that far away. I need to attract their attention so they will give chase. The pit will do the rest."

She stares at me.

"A sand pit? Are you sure? There's so much that can go wrong."

"I have much experience," I reply patiently. "I believe this to be safer then pushing forward."

She sighs. "I really don't like this."

"I know," I say softly.

She nods after another moment.

"Okay," she says in a small voice. When she looks back up at me, there is clear concern in her eyes. "Just be careful, okay?"

I smile, cupping the side of her face. It is nice to be so cared for. I know my brothers care, but their care is a harder thing, more pragmatic. They know what I am capable of. And they also know sometimes we must all put ourselves at risk for the greater good.

"I will be exceptionally careful," I reassure her. "I have you to come back to, after all."

She smiles at that, rolling her eyes.

"That is such a line," she says.

"A line?" I question, frowning. "What do you mean?"

She blushes, looking away.

"Never mind. It doesn't matter. Just come back as quickly as you can, okay?"

"Yes. I will come back as soon as I safely can." I do not want her to worry. Nor do I want to leave her unprotected for longer than absolutely necessary.

I lean down and kiss her lips softly. The sooner we do this, the sooner I can be back with her.

"Now. The best place to hide you is right here."

Confused, she looks around. There is nothing but sand all around us.

"Right here?" she repeats dubiously.

"Yes. I have hidden in the sand many times. Trust me."

She looks down at the sand. "If you say so," she mutters, clearly not convinced.

She doesn't appear any more convinced as I start to dig out a hole at the base of one of the nearby dunes.

"Sit down here," I say gesturing towards the small hole.

"Okay. I'm trusting you," she adds, clearly not comfortable as she lies down in the shallow hole. "Now what?"

"Now I will pour sand over you."

I proceed to do just that, covering her entire body, leaving space for her face.

"Are you comfortable?" I ask, stepping back to critique my handiwork.

I start to level out some areas with my hands so they will not be as noticeable.

She looks at me incredulously.

"I'm buried in sand. I'm not comfortable."

I chuckle.

"Can you remain here for a bit of time?" I ask instead, rephrasing my question.

She wiggles under the blanket of sand, attempting to get more comfortable.

"Yeah, I guess. Just try not to take too long."

I nod, leaning down to kiss her cheek.

"I will hurry. It will not take me long."

With that promise in mind, I take the cart and push it over to where the oasis is.

Once there, I take out various pieces of the glass that we have collected and carefully start to cover the sandpit. I take my time setting the first one down cautiously, checking to be sure it will not sink. It does not, floating at the top quite easily. Good.

It takes a while to make the pattern appear random and not so suspicious. I even take the time to sprinkle meteorite glass around the pit itself, not concentrating only in the center of the area. I'm conscious the whole time of Nora, waiting for me, buried in the sand, and I have to fight to be careful and not rush, or I could fall into the sandpit myself.

Finally, I can step back and survey my handiwork. The

sunlight glints off the various pieces of glass, completely obscuring the variation in the sand there. Perfect.

I take the cart and hide it behind a tree. Then it is time to go back to the invaders. I travel back over the sand quickly, not bothering to be stealthy this time. I want them to hear me. Because I do not have to be quiet, I make it back to their encampment much more quickly.

I do not want my appearance to seem staged, so I decide to run directly into their camp as though I was not expecting them to be there. Taking a deep breath, I flare my wings out and force my body to a stop, my feet digging into the sand halfway down one of the surrounding dunes.

They all turn to me as one.

A staccato yell erupts from the group. I turn around and run away as though startled by their sudden appearance.

I do not move too fast, slowing my run until I hear them coming after me. When I do hear multiple footsteps, I increase my speed again. I need to be enough distance away from them that their stunners cannot hit me, but close enough that they have no chance of losing me.

My focus is razor sharp as I lead them away from where I know I have hidden Nora. This is to keep her safe. I will not make a mistake.

I crest another rise and see the oasis, the sun shining off of the glass. It acts as a marker for me to aim at. Switching directions, I run directly for it.

In order to lure them into the pit, I have to run over it myself. Or at least give the appearance of running over it. Judging the distance carefully—I do not want to end up stuck in the pit myself—I flare my wings out, ready to leap. I cannot look like I am leaping too high or they will look to see what I am trying to avoid.

So I jump just enough to help me glide but not rise too far over the sand, just barely managing to make it over the pit. I land so close that my feet sink into the edge of it and I stumble forward.

I do not stop running, using the momentum to propel me onward.

They are directly behind me, but all of them must keep running long enough that those in the back of the group also sink into the pit.

So I do not slow down, not until I hear the cries change behind me. When I look back, all of the invaders are in the pit, those who were at the head of the group sinking faster. Those in the back were clearly running much too fast and too close to the others to heed their quicker counterparts' cries in time. They are struggling so hard that they have already buried themselves halfway into the sandpit.

They are occupied sufficiently, so I return to the oasis to retrieve the cart. The cries of alarm continue to ring in the air as I turn and run back towards Nora.

I do not have to watch to know that they are doomed. War is a messy business, but I stifle my compassion. They were the ones who decided to invade our planet. We are within our rights to defend ourselves.

When I make it back to Nora, I immediately push the sand off of her. She lifts her arms out when the weight decreases, and I take hold of her hands, helping her rise up out of the hole. I start to brush the sand off her, but she does not wait to be clean, throwing her arms around me in a fierce hug. I wrap my own around her, holding her close. She trembles with relief.

"I was so worried," she murmurs against my chest. "There were so many things that could've gone wrong, so many things I kept thinking about. And I knew there wasn't really anything I could do if you didn't come back..."

I kiss the top of her head.

"Life is a risk," I murmur. "However, in this case I was not in that much danger. Brawn is not always the answer. There is also wit."

I tap my temple sagely when she pulls back to look up at me.

"Wit, huh?"

"I have much wit," I say with a serious face. "Apparently more wit than ten invaders combined."

Her mouth twitches. And then she starts to chuckle.

"You're right. I don't know why I was worried at all," she says, shaking her head.

"Yes," I agree. "You must see that I am greatly powerful. Invaders are no match for me," I add, deliberately exaggerating my tone and my stance. Her laugh at the idiotic display is my reward. I grin back, happy to see her calm again.

She becomes serious again when we turn towards the cart.

"Do you know who they are?" she asks as we move to travel once more.

I know she is referring to the invaders. I sigh, shaking my head in genuine regret.

"I loathe the missing pieces of memory," I admit. Even the Order has a few missing pieces after the Devastation. "There is something familiar about their scent, but I simply cannot recall what it is." I shake my head. "It is quite frustrating."

"I can't help but feel that we're going to find out soon," she says.

"Perhaps."

It is a reality that the invaders do not seem to be leaving Tajss anytime soon. I am not certain we will learn anymore, but we might have ample opportunity to do so. Whether that information will be helpful or not is yet to be seen. In any case, I do not want to linger in the area in case more of their kind arrive, bringing more trouble for us. To that end, I push us forward.

Luckily, we have not actually traveled that far away from the Tribe. Even with the cart and with Nora's slower pace, we manage to arrive at the Tribe's stronghold by nightfall without encountering any more obstacles.

"Thank God," Nora says as the wall comes into sight.

I nod my agreement. I would much rather have Nora here behind the safety of the wall, enclosed in the protection of the Tribe, even if the Elders are suspicious of me. I brace myself for it, though.

When we walk past the barrier of the wall, we are greeted by the other Zmaj and the human females having dinner.

"Oh my God, we were just about to send out people for you!"

"And you were able to bring back glass!"

"Where were you two holed up? We couldn't find you anywhere!"

Nora explains what happened, how we had to take cover. When she pauses to take a breath, I deliberately step to her side and wrap an arm around her. She stiffens slightly looking up at me with a question in her eyes, but she does not resist when I draw her into a kiss in front of everyone.

"I will take the cart to the collection area," I say to her after I pull back from her soft lips. Nora nods, slightly dazed.

I smile internally as I push the cart away. I hear the murmurs start immediately. Good. I want everyone to know Nora is my mate, that she is taken.

I feel the heavy stares of the Elders upon me as I move, but I ignore them. Unless and until they speak to me directly, it is not an issue I will deal with.

I drop the cart off and return to the kitchen area to find Nora still there, gossiping with her friends. Her very interested female friends.

"Oh my God, that's so romantic!"

"Yeah, it's like a Lifetime movie! You guys were holed up in a cave and fell in love! It's so sweet I could gag!"

"Nora, this is so great—I'm so happy for you!"

"Yeah, he is pretty wonderful," Nora agrees, blushing under the attention, but also glimmering with happiness. I feel my own chest fill with emotion for her.

Having heard enough, I step closer to Nora. The conversation halts as everyone realizes I'm there. I nod at her friends as I take Nora's hand in mine.

"I believe it is time to withdraw for the night," I say to her.

Nora blushes even more, but does not pull away. She turns readily to leave with me.

"Bye, guys," she throws over her shoulder.

"Bye, Nora!" her friends chorus all together, giggling.

She ducks her head in shyness, but does not deny their obvious assumption as I draw her over to my own chambers. They are correct after all.

Once we are alone, I pull her back into my arms.

"Now that we are alone, I want to take my time with you," I inform her softly, leaning down to kiss her cheeks, her forehead, her small nose.

She sighs, sinking in against me. "Yes, please."

I chuckle under my breath, pushing her down towards my pallet. And I do take my time.

Stripping both of us first, I kiss every inch of her body, from the top of her head down to the soles of her feet. She is so perfect. I do not think I could ever sate myself on her. I would forever want more. Her soft skin, her delicate scent, the curves and give of her body. I bury my face against her breasts, luxuriating in their softness, in the rapid beat of her heart.

When I reach the down between her legs, I find her wet and welcoming, but I do not sink into her right away. I turn her over and kiss every inch of her back too. From the nape of her neck, to the small of her back, to the curves under her backside and the backs of her knees, until she is wiggling with impatience underneath me.

"Archion," she complains, her voice breathy with arousal.

Grinning, I lower my body over hers and sink into her from behind. She gasps as I groan, the wet clasp of her familiar but still so new. So glorious. The coupling is just as stunning as before. She makes me feel things beyond the physical, like we are becoming one with each other, the lines between us blurring as pleasure drenches us. It takes some effort to hold myself back, to wait until she reaches her peak, but then I allow myself to reach it as well.

I wonder how this treasure has entered my life. How I am lucky enough to be holding this perfection of a female, to be holding Nora. To have her in my life.

We fall asleep with me still inside of her.

And when I wake in the middle of the night, I find myself hard and still inside her sweet body. When I start to move, she awakens sleepily. I reach between us to rub at her small nub and she cries out, the orgasm quick and sharp. Moaning, I roll onto my back and settle her on top of me.

We fall asleep once more, but not for the last time. I lose count of the times we couple during that night. I know I will never forget it. And, by the end of it, I am more certain than ever that I will never be able to satiate myself with her.

I will always want another taste.

## 16

## NORA

*a*rchion kisses me awake the next morning. I hum my enjoyment. I could really get used to this.

"I am going to go on patrol," he tells me in that deep voice that sends shivers through me. "I hope your day is a good one."

I smile as I stretch. "I hope you have a good day, too."

He kisses me again and then leaves. I'm pretty sure he's going to be early, but that doesn't surprise me. I doubt Archion is ever anything but responsible.

The wake-up call has me jumping out of bed with a smile on my face, ready for the day. Maybe it's dangerous to feel so invested in this still-unlabeled relationship, but I can't help it. I'm going take what happiness I can get.

I'm still riding that high when Addison comes to visit the Tribe that afternoon. All of the girls get together at lunch to talk with her, to catch up.

Since she's the tech expert, we're all interested in what she has to say about the glass and the meteors we found after that beautiful light show in the sky.

"Actually, we're not all that sure how to use it," Addison

admits as we eat. "The glass is definitely different, but we're still trying to learn more about it."

That sends a ripple of interest through us. We've all been really careful to collect all the glass that melted the sand within our territories, but it's still unclear if the invaders have collected their own from other meteorite showers elsewhere.

Not knowing what the glass actually does adds another wrinkle to everything.

"Has Errol learned anything?" I ask, curious.

Addison nods.

"There is a sound frequency imprinted in the glass. But that's not all that unusual. He's found the same thing to be true with some of the ores that come from the mining settlement."

Interesting. We talk over the meteorite showers some more, and the glass. All of this could mean changes in how we do things right now. Not that everything isn't always in some state of flux. We have to figure things out as we go. Addison also brings us some news from the city, which is nice.

But towards the end, the talk somehow turns towards me.

"Enough about all of that stuff." Addison leans in towards me, her eyes sparkling. "I hear you're with Archion now, Nora. Come on, spill."

I blush as the other girls share knowing glances.

"Uh, yes? We kind of got together when we were trapped out in the desert during that sandstorm," I say quickly. Maybe that'll be enough to appease her.

But I see Addison open her mouth to ask something else, and it might be more personal.

Delilah takes pity on me before she can, standing with her dishes in hand.

"All right guys. Let her go—I need help in the kitchen."

The girls protest, but I get up with a silent, relieved sigh, and follow Delilah into the kitchen. We need to start prep for the next meal.

"Thank you," I murmur to Delilah as I work alongside her.

"No problem," she reassures me. But then she gives me a sidelong glance. "Though, if you do want to talk to some-body...you know I'm here, right?"

I chuckle, recognizing her tactful attempt to talk about the same subject. Of course, I'm much more comfortable now, alone with her. I know she genuinely cares and we've grown really close working together. I'm happy to share.

"Well, we had to find shelter when the sandstorm got so strong. With the close proximity and the enforced interac-tion...I guess we just couldn't avoid it anymore."

Delilah nods.

"That makes sense. We should have found a way to isolate you two earlier—it was clear to anyone who had eyes that you guys were into each other." She stops what she's doing to give me a warm hug. "I'm really glad that this happened."

I blush, considering that as I hug her back.

"Were we really that obvious?" I ask, uncomfortable.

"Yes. But it was adorable." She waves her hand. "Never mind that. What happened after the sandstorm?"

"Well, he trained me with the shock-stick, tried to help me learn how to protect myself. And then, later, he went out while we were smoking meat and came back with a flower for me."

"A flower?" she says. "Well, then. That is romantic! Guy knows what he's doing."

I smile, nodding.

"It was the first time we kissed," I admit, sighing over the memory.

Maybe I'm being insufferable, but I'm allowed when it's still so new, right?

"Oh, that sounds just about perfect. Then what?"

"Well, we went out to collect glass, there was an meteorite shower..."

I describe what happened next, skimming over details, but I can see Delilah put two and two together. I appreciate that she doesn't tease me over it.

"I'm so happy for you Nora. And judging by how things are going, you might just have some dragonlings of your own faster than you think," she points out, wagging her eyebrows at me.

Okay, there goes the no teasing. I flush a bright pink, just in time for the little ones to run into the kitchen.

"Nora! Nora!" they call out, running over to hug me. I crouch down to hug them back, taking in their sweet baby scents.

And, for the first time in a long time, I feel that almost-forgotten hope rekindle inside me. If Archion asks me to be his mate, I'm going to say yes.

And I will be happy—so happy—to give him as many dragonlings as my body can make.

# 17

## ARCHION

$\mathcal{I}$ come back from patrol, making my way towards my quarters. I do not know what the Elders are planning, but they are holding back for now. Keeping their own counsel. Perhaps my meeting with the Commander was helpful. I do not know. I am going to have to think about—

My head jerks up as I hear an odd sound ahead. It is coming from my quarters. Rushing forward, I pull back the curtain and step inside.

It's Samil, one of the younger members of the Tribe, rifling through my belongings. He dares?

My bijass rushes to the surface, a tinge of red coating my vision as I take a step forward and grab him by the scruff of his neck, fiery rage burning in my gut.

His eyes are wide with shock at the abrupt attack. Their training is weak.

"What are you doing?" I snarl.

Not waiting for an answer, I grab him as he turns and throw him against the wall. He hits with a satisfying thud and is momentarily stunned. Shaking it off, he raises his fists to defend himself.

He's young and his clumsy defense tells me he's not well trained. He swings but I dodge it easily, striking his arm as it passes me, attacking the meaty muscle. I know well the effect of such a blow. Numbing, painful, and as I expect he cries out and his arm drops to his side.

He doesn't stop, to his credit, swinging his tail at my feet while punching with his good arm. It's clumsy but brave. Jumping over his tail I twist, intending to stun his remaining arm with another strike. Somehow he sees my move and his fist changes directions, connecting with my jaw.

Pain explodes with his contact and my bijass roars as I stumble back from the blow.

I hear cries from outside, and know the battle is no longer a secret, but I do not care. The bijass has a firm hold of me as I grab my lochaber from where I dropped it upon entering. Bringing it up and over in a single sweeping motion I lower it between us, ready to run him through.

He wipes at the blood dripping from his mouth. His lochaber is across the cave. I see his eyes dart towards it as I near him. I'll cut him down well before he reaches it. I grip my weapon. I know exactly where I will swing, how hard the blow must be to be fatal.

"Archion! No!"

I pause. The other dragon uses the instant to dive and roll for his lochaber, coming to his feet gripping it in an awkwardly--

The voice is Nora's. The only voice that could possibly cut through the bijass like this. The panic in it snaps me back to my senses, my duty and training swiftly rising to the fore once more, helping me beat the bijass back down. I take a step back from my opponent, my chest heaving as I forcefully calm myself down.

I look to the entrance. Nora stands there, her eyes wide as she looks from me to Samil.

"Archion," she whispers hoarsely, horrified. Her eyes are worried.

And then I know exactly why. In the next instant, other Zmaj rush in, the commotion loud around me. I stand there calmly, allowing them to divest me of my lochaber, my eyes still on Nora. I understand their desire to restrain me.

"The Elders will deal with him," Padraig mutters.

I never move my gaze from Nora. I speak to her without ever opening my mouth, telling her I will return. They will not keep me away from her. The slight nod she gives me lets me know that she understands, and that she has no doubt that I will be back.

I have to break our silent communication when I am dragged out of my quarters, out to the common area where much of the Tribe watches. Their gazes vary from suspicious, to angry, to concerned.

I am taken to that same cavern where I spoke to the Elders before. Kalessin and Falkosh are already waiting, their faces tense.

"You dare attack one of the Tribe while you are here under our hospitality?" Kalessin begins, his voice too loud, too brash.

"If your hospitality includes searching my things, you do not know what hospitality means."

I make sure to keep my voice calm, measured. I cannot allow them to rattle me. Not when I just regained control.

"You do not give us any answers!" Falkosh returns, frustration infusing his voice. "How do you expect us to trust you if you do not trust us enough to provide us with the answers we need?"

"There are things I cannot speak of," I say simply.

That does not appease them.

"You must tell us where you are from. You must tell us

who your people are," Kalessin orders, his voice grating on the ears.

I remain silent. I will not speak a word of the Order. I would need to report back, ask permission before I ever could. I will take my own life before I say anything, if they force me to.

The Order survives because the hearts of the dragons who are members are among the most noble in the land. An undying, secret tradition. Worth more than my life alone.

"If you do not answer us, we will be forced to assume that you are an enemy," Kalessin tries, changing his tact.

"If you were more open, we would not look through your belongings," Falkosh repeats once more. "Do you not see, do you not understand that we need to know more?"

"We must protect our people!"

"I understand that." I pause, meeting each of their eyes. "Because I must also protect my own."

That gives them pause. But they still continue on with the questions, their frustration growing.

Still, I am not even remotely swayed from my original position. I will not give them any information no matter what.

Eventually, they tire of grilling me, the anger and frustration marking their faces harshly.

"Padraig, take him to his room. Have guards placed in front." Kalessin turns to me as Padraig nods, gesturing to the Zmaj apparently waiting for that order. "As we are not yet certain you are not a threat to us, we are going to ask you not to leave."

I know it is not a request, so I say nothing. I am escorted back to my quarters. They close the curtain, and I hear them take up positions directly outside. They think to hold me prisoner here.

Growling to myself, I finally allow myself to show my

agitation, pacing around the small space. If they knew my rank, they would never dare such a thing. Of course, they do not. They know nothing.

The Zmaj of the Tribe and the Zmaj of the city, all are veiled in ignorance.

## 18

## NORA

*M*y stomach is in knots the next day when Archion is let back out into the communal area. This whole thing is such a mess, and I have no idea how to deal with any of it. It's what everybody's talking about right now, despite the everyday dangers that are always going on in the background. It's too juicy not to be the center of conversation. Doesn't mean it isn't still uncomfortable to be around.

When Samil stands up at Archion's appearance, my heart starts to beat faster.

"Why are you letting him out?" he asks, eyeing Archion warily.

Archion does not lose his cool, though the temper flares in his eyes as he faces the dragon he fought earlier.

"I was not the instigator," Archion points out. "Perhaps you should keep your hands to yourself rather than putting them upon other people's property."

"What is it that you are trying to hide?" Samil retorts, stepping closer to Archion.

Oh no. What is Samil doing?

"That is none of your business," Archion growls, meeting him step for step.

"I do not trust you. And I do not know why you are still allowed here behind the wall," Samil sneers. "We have been too soft with you."

And then he punches Archion in the face.

I watch in horror, my mouth hanging open in shock. What the hell!

Triggered, Archion doesn't hold back. He grabs his opponent and the two grapple.

Everyone cries out now, rushing forward to stop the fight. The dragons are torn apart by other Zmaj. Couldn't they have done that a little earlier?

"He needs to be exiled!" Samil growls. "He is dangerous!"

Inga has come and stood by her mate's side, holding his arm.

"Perhaps Samil is right," Falkosh says, coming out with his fellow Elder at the noise. "We do not need a disruption such as this. Not now when threats loom on the horizon."

"Really?!" I exclaim. When all of the shouts and voices quiet down, I realize I said that last bit out loud. But I'm so beyond frustrated at this point, I don't even care that all eyeballs are on me. I look out at the gathered crowd, at the Elders. "Don't cast Archion out for rightfully defending his belongings! He had a right to be angry. And he didn't instigate this confrontation right now either—Samil very publicly provoked him!"

A beat of silence as everyone absorbs that.

But the Elders don't address me.

"What are you hiding?" Kalessin asks Archion, stepping forward.

"That is the real question here," Falkosh agrees.

From all over the common room come voices that back up that same sentiment. I stand there, unable to defend him on this point. He hasn't even told me anything, and I understand exactly how suspicious that looks.

I look over at Archion, at a loss. I want to protect him, but I don't have any ammunition for this line of questioning. Archion looks angry, but it's back to a controlled anger now.

"I have aided you," he responds into the tense silence. "You are well aware of that. That is all you need to know." There are some restless murmurs that arise at that. Archion continues after they settle down. "I will, however, have a word with Visidion. If he will entertain me."

I've never seen anyone stand up to the Elders like this. I feel fear in my heart, even as I admire the boldness of his defiance. It's completely unprecedented, at least in my own experience.

He's simply more committed to keeping his secrets than adhering to accepted behavior in the Tribe. I hold my breath along with everyone else, waiting to see how the Elders will react. Their desperation is clear in their answer.

"Very well," Falkosh agrees, eyeing Archion. "We will grant you leave to go to the city. With an escort, of course."

I swallow, my stomach still clenched with nerves. It's as if they want to know what Archion is hiding more than they want food or water or a safe place to sleep. I just hope this resolves things somehow.

How can Archion and I be together if he's not even welcome here? It's a question I don't have the answer to.

## 19

### ARCHION

*M*y guard escorts me back to my quarters.

I hope speaking with Visidion will settle this matter, but I am not at all certain. I think about how to approach the upcoming meeting with him while I gather my belongings.

If the matter is not settled soon, the bad blood will only grow, as evidenced by the confrontation in the communal area today. No matter how much in the right I might be, I am certain the other members of the Tribe will not take kindly to me fighting with their own.

Glancing over to ensure the curtain is still closed, I move over to the shadowed corner on one side, reaching behind the rock where I stored the scroll.

After being here for so long, it just was not safe or practical to carry it around with me constantly, so I began to hide it in this corner. I take it out, giving it a quick once-over before I pack it away again. This was the reason why I was so enraged. I was so relieved when I found it safe its spot, undisturbed. They did not find it when they sent their spy.

"Archion?" Nora is ducking in through the curtain, her

eyes immediately going to the scroll in my hands. I do not hurry to hide it. She already saw it. I do decide to tuck it away again. The eyes of my beloved tell me that she will not speak a word of having glimpsed it. She understands me, is able to read my eyes and sense the scroll's importance. There is no female more suited for me than she. I put the scroll back in its hiding spot and rise to my feet.

"Nora," I whisper, reaching out for her.

She swallows, looking up at me with desperate eyes, the same desperation I feel. When I lift her up and brace her against the wall, she wraps her legs and arms around me, meeting my kiss with her own demands.

The desire and the fear that we both feel permeates every touch. I try to shove away the fear, try to help her exorcise it as well. The future is uncertain, but we have now.

She breaks the kiss, her hands cupping my face.

"Archion, I'm afraid," she whispers.

Her vulnerability hurts me. I wish I could protect her from all things that would scare and harm her.

"Everything will be fine," I murmur, willing it to be so. "For now, we have each other."

"Yes," she whispers, blinking back tears. She kisses me, channeling all of that raw emotion into the meeting of lips.

I am undone. I do not take her to the pallet. That is not the kind of joining we need at this moment. Quickly, I take off her pants and mine, releasing my erection. I lift her back up and she wraps her legs around me. With one hand, I stroke her sweet girl fur, and between her folds, I find her wet and welcoming.

Groaning in relief, I thrust into her heated sheath in the next instant. She cries out, arching against me.

I kiss the beautiful curve of her neck, taking a deep breath at the sensation of her wrapped around me. I need this. For more than just now.

I revel in our joining, but I am still fearful that it may just be this time. No. I push the thought aside. I refuse to think so negatively.

I grip her jaw, tilting her face to kiss her again, the taste of her, the feel of her, a necessary reprieve.

Nora is my mate, my home.

I move inside her, her small cries, her moans urging me on. It is a bit rough, a bit raw. What we both need to ground us in all this uncertainty.

When she reaches her pleasure, I push myself deeper into her, watching her face as my own overtakes me.

She is flushed, her eyes closed tightly, her teeth sinking into her lower lip. Gorgeous. I have never seen a more beautiful sight.

But I am not yet finished. I pull out of her, I help her get to her feet, and then I turn her around and brace her against the wall.

"Archion?" she asks, looking over her shoulder, her eyes still dazed from pleasure.

Tilting her hips, I sink back into her with my second cock. She gasps, pushing back against me, her head resting against my shoulder. I take her all over again.

She is mine.

No matter what happens, I will never let her go.

## 20

## NORA

*A*rawn and Padraig take us in the rover to the city. The damn thing bounces around so much I'm sure my spine is a mess. There's not a lot of handholds and I keep bouncing up against Archion. As I'm smashed into him again, my breasts crushing against the hard muscles of his chest, my nipples betray me, hardening as last night drifts through my thoughts. He grabs onto me, holding me tight, and I wish, with all my heart, we were alone.

I insisted on coming, refusing to allow them to take Archion anywhere alone. After everything that's happened, I guess I just don't trust anyone not to hurt him. Maybe I can't physically stop someone, but I'm hoping my presence is at least a deterrent.

"Visidion is going to want to see you right away," Arawn comments, looking back to meet Archion's eyes. "I know you made a good impression on him earlier."

Archion inclines his head. "Thank you. The Commander seemed to be a reasonable leader."

Arawn smiles, facing forward once more.

"That he is," he says.

Padraig remains mostly silent, but Arawn continues to engage in sporadic conversation with both Archion and me. He is a lot less gruff than the others have been with Archion. After a few minutes, it's clear that he agrees with Archion about what has happened, that he sides with him, though he can't say as much.

I agree. The Elders had no right to send someone to search through Archion's belongings. It was underhanded, disrespectful, and a clear show of distrust. How can they expect Archion to trust them with his secret if they couldn't even show enough restraint not to search his things?

In my opinion, it was a terrible precedent to set if they really wanted to build a potential alliance.

As I listen to Arawn talk to Archion, I feel a bit of relief. I've been beside myself over what the other dragons might have planned for Archion. I saw the anger, saw the desire to push him back when he got into that second fight with Samil.

Reason isn't in control with the Zmaj, not when their territorial natures are triggered. I was worried in the beginning when the Elders watched Archion with such a suspicion. Now everyone is walking on eggshells around Archion after the hubbub of the last day or two, though he doesn't seem to be moved by it all, showing no indication of his own emotions about the subject.

I look over at his profile. In some ways, he's stoic to the core. Yeah, he's been soft and caring with me. But I see a much more practical side of him with others, and with situations in general.

Honestly, seeing him not rattled sets me more at ease. It's nice to be around an energy that's calmer than my own. It helps me steady myself. The ride to the city seems both too long and too short at the same time. I don't like waiting for the other shoe to drop, but I also don't know what we're going to find in the city. Is it going to be more hostility? Are we just going from the pan into the fire? I have no idea.

Luckily, when Padraig parks the rover and we get out to go into the city, it doesn't seem like anybody has it in for us at all. We're immediately led to our room. Together. Looks like news of Archion and me reached the city before us.

But we don't have much time to sit in the room and wait. Arawn knocks on the door and ducks his head in.

"Visidion is ready to see you," he announces.

Archion nods, turning to me.

"I will be back soon," he murmurs, leaning down to kiss me lightly.

I nod. I clearly haven't been asked to join, which is all right with me. I don't know if I can help the situation.

I watch him leave, then sit back down on the bed, completely at loose ends. What are they going to do?

What if Visidion tells Archion he has to leave right away? Would they even let me know? Or would they just toss him out?

I sit there, ruminating over that.

Okay. Obviously, I can't be left here alone with my thoughts. I will self-destruct with enough time. I leave the room and start down the hall with the intention of seeking out the girls. I could really do with some girl time right now.

Luckily, when I go out into the courtyard outside, I see a group of them sitting and chatting. Lana, Calista, Jolie, and Amara all greet me with smiles.

"Nora, hey!"

"Hi, Nora!"

"Come join us!"

I smile, making my way over to them and taking an open seat.

"I'd ask you what brings you here, but the rumor mill has been swirling," Amara says directly. She isn't the type to beat around the bush, which I can appreciate.

"Yeah," I sigh. "The Elders have been pushing Archion to spill the beans about his people. And he is just that determined to keep everything close to his chest."

"That's difficult," Calista murmurs, her eyes sympathetic. "I'm sorry."

I nod. "Thank you."

"I'm sure everything will be fine," Lana says, reaching out to pat my hand. "Visidion is a reasonable kind of guy. Archion hasn't done anything terrible."

"What exactly did happen?" Jolie asks. "I'm not sure if the news hit us in its entirety, to be honest. It's like getting a story through a long game of telephone."

I chuckle, shaking my head. I know what she means.

"The Elders ordered Archion's rooms searched. He didn't appreciate it."

Amara nods.

"I wouldn't either," she comments. "And that makes no sense. If you want an alliance with someone, that's definitely not the right way to go about it."

"I'm glad someone agrees with me," I say wryly.

"Guys, maybe we should talk about something else right now," Calista interjects, watching my face. No doubt I look just as worried as I feel. "So, how did you and Archion get together?"

The question, the glitter of curiosity in her eyes, has me laughing.

"Well, it all started with a sandstorm..."

I exhaust the subject of how Archion and I got together. Which is truly a testament to how much I don't want to think about the meeting he's in. Then I switch the subject over to them in an effort to continue not thinking about it.

"Well, Illadon is doing amazing, but he's also driving me right up the wall! You'll never believe..." I relax a little, listening to Calista talk about her child.

But it doesn't take my mind completely off Archion.

I don't know if anything can.

## 21

## ARCHION

*I* leave Nora behind, following Arawn and Padraig to Visidion's office. As I leave, I have to calm the fear that they won't allow me to come back to her. They could try—but they would never succeed. Settling that surety around me like armor, I face the Tribe Commander.

Visidion is just as imposing as I remember him being. His laser-sharp gaze focuses upon me as we walk inside, the door closing behind us.

He doesn't break the silence for a couple of moments, allowing it to settle around us.

"I suppose these are not the most ideal circumstances in which to meet once more," he finally says in that calm, measured voice.

I shake my head. "No."

The corner of his mouth tilts up as he stands and walks out from behind his desk.

"I hear that you requested a meeting with me," he says, watching me. "Why was that?"

"I thought perhaps you would be willing to listen to what I had to say," I respond.

He raises his eyebrows at me.

"And the Tribe Elders were not willing to listen?" he asks. "I was under the impression that they were willing to listen to anything you had to say."

"Perhaps. But when someone decides to breach my trust, I am disinclined to be open. Or helpful."

Visidion nods, his smile fading. "I cannot say that I do not understand."

"I thought perhaps you would understand about matters of honor. And also, perhaps you would be willing to entertain the possibility of an alliance against the invaders."

That has him straightening and taking notice.

"An alliance?" he repeats.

"Yes. A very valuable one."

He shakes his head.

"How do I know that alliance would be a valuable one?" he asks. "You have not revealed any useful information about where you come from, about who your people are. What if you do not have good intentions? What if your people do not have good intentions? I am certain you can understand my reticence."

It is a fair point. "I am a member of a group called the Order," I explain carefully. I need to give him enough information to assuage his fears, but not so much that I compromise my own oath. "It is a very old and honorable institution."

He nods slowly, listening.

"Is everyone in this Order as well trained as you are?" he asks.

Visidion has not seen me fight, but I am not surprised that he has asked others in the Tribe about me.

"Yes," I say simply.

His eyes narrow, most likely thinking about the danger

that we could represent if we are enemies rather than possible allies. He should consider that possibility.

"How many are in this Order?"

"That I cannot say. I have my loyalties to consider as well."

He nods, moving to the next question.

"What reassurance can you give me that the Order is of a sympathetic mind? Because you will have to provide some sort of reasonable reassurance. Allowing you to speak with the rest of your group after you know so much about us...you can see how that is a risk for us."

I nod. That is also fair.

"If my intentions were not good, I could have easily left the group I first met to fight the invaders alone. I could have also left them to fight the two other beasts on the way back to their cave system." I shake my head. "I have risked my life to aid the Tribe. If I only wanted information, I could have followed them home and simply watched. But I did not." I raise my hands, letting them drop once more. "I have honored them, honored the rules of their home. Only to have my trust breached. Rather than respecting my own boundaries, they decided to take matters into their own hands. My question for you would be—why should *we* trust *you*?" I look back at Arawn and Padraig. "It seems as though I am now a prisoner simply for protecting myself, for protecting my property."

The silence after that pronouncement is deep.

Visidion watches me, his mind working quickly behind his gaze. I do not know if I have succeeded articulating my point well.

"Why are you so adamant about an alliance?" Visidion asks, not addressing what I just said.

I let out a huff of breath. "By now it has become obvious that the invaders are not leaving. It is also obvious that they are a threat to all of us left here on Tajss. It is only prudent and intelligent to combine forces against the common enemy." I spread out my arms. "Our objectives are matched in this matter. I understand that there is risk involved. But sometimes, one must move forward on faith."

He watches me, leaning back against his desk, tapping his fingers on the top as he thinks.

"You make a convincing argument," he finally says. "If I were to consider this, how would you propose we meet with your Order?"

I have already thought of this, thought of the best way to present this to minimize risk for them.

"I can lead you close to their territory," I say. It is not a lie —he simply does not know that there are multiple territories. "With an escort, of course," I add, nodding back at Arawn and Padraig.

"And how will we reach out to them?" Visidion pushes.

"If we are close enough to the edge of our territory, someone will see us. We will not be left alone for long, not after they recognize me," I explain.

"You are confident of this?"

"I am. And when the one of my brothers arrives, I can pose the possibility of a meeting between the Order and the city. A meeting to discuss mutual enemies and any possible trade that might be had." I bow my head slightly. "Assuming I am granted permission to make such arrangements, of course."

Another pause as Visidion processes my proposal.

"You will speak to whoever arrives in front of your escort."

I nod. I understand his trepidation. I know the location of both the Tribe and the city.

"Yes, of course."

Visidion sighs. "Archion, I am going to place my trust in you. I hope it is not in vain."

I feel excitement build but retain an outwardly calm façade.

"You will not regret it."

## 22

### NORA

*W*hen Archion returns to me in one piece, I'm overjoyed. He's safe. I want to throw myself into his arms and twirl around like in the vids.

Also, Visidion has agreed to meet with the Order to talk about a possible alliance. The outcome is so much better than I could have even hoped for.

Of course, just as I feel relief settling in, and we take a moment to eat, trouble comes knocking. Typical.

I hear the ripple go through the crowd before Visidion shows up, a small army of Zmaj already behind him.

"There is trouble at the perimeter of the city," he announces, looking over the crowd. "Noncombatants should go inside until we take care of the matter." I see Visidion's eyes fall on Archion, and I know what he's going to say before he says it. "Archion, will you join our ranks?"

"Yes," he agrees without hesitation. Also a response I could have predicted. He would have joined them even if Visidion hadn't asked.

My heart clenches and my stomach turns over. I don't

want him to go into danger. Then again, where and when on Tajss is danger far away?

Archion turns to me, cupping the side of my face and capturing my lips with his in a hard kiss. When he breaks it, he meets my eyes.

"I promise to return, Nora," he murmurs, for my ears only.

I try to smile. "You better." He smiles at me, kissing me again before standing and joining Visidion's group.

I watch him walk away—towards a battle.

Worry beats at me, a familiar but heightened feeling in this case. We finally found a sanctuary and now this. I've been so stressed out, I feel the urge to just curl up and start crying now.

I take a deep breath, trying to control myself, to control my emotions. I'm usually very good at keeping my head these days, but that was before I found something as profound and soul-shaking as what I have with Archion. I'm desperately afraid of losing him. I never realized how fearful I could be until now, until I have something so precious to lose.

I head back to our apartment almost in a daze, trying to keep it together. When I get there, I just curl up in bed, trying not to think about anything. I'm not at all successful.

At one point, there's a knock at the door. It's Calista and the rest of the girls.

"Can we come in?" she asks when I open the door. She holds up a plate. "We come bearing food and drink."

I smile at her wanly, stepping back and opening the door wider to let them all in.

"Sure."

They all give me sympathetic looks as they march in, holding plates and bottles.

"There is no point in worrying about it," Amara says, not

unkindly. "This is kind of a fact of life here. And the Zmaj are exceedingly good at battle. I'd bet money on them any day."

"I know. But I can't stop worrying." Nothing but having him back with me will stop that.

"Oh, sweetie," Amara murmurs, giving me a hug. "Here, food always helps me."

"And gossip," Jolie adds.

I laugh, taking the cup of wine Amara hands over to me.

"Some alcohol doesn't hurt either."

Amen to that. I take a sip and settle in.

"Thanks for coming guys," I say, looking around the circle of friendly faces. "It means a lot."

"We have to stick together," Calista says. "All we have here is one another."

I appreciate the sentiment. And she's right. We need to hold each other down. So we talk. Or, more accurately, they talk and I mostly listen, eating and drinking.

It's really sweet of them to come and try to get my mind off things, to distract me from my worry. It's partially successful, distracting me enough that I don't feel like my heart is going to beat out of my chest, but there is no way to completely push aside thoughts of Archion and what he's facing out there. Eventually, all of us start to tire. When I yawn, covering my mouth, Amara finally stands up.

"I think it's time to call it a night, girls," she announces. "Sleep is knocking."

I nod while everyone else agrees.

"I'm right down the hall if you need me," Calista offers. "We all are."

I walk them the few steps to the door and smile at them, feeling my heart warm.

"Thanks guys. It means a lot."

A minute later, we've all said our goodbyes and hugged each other. I'm alone in the room again. Sighing, I climb into bed, not at all optimistic about actually sleeping. And I'm not wrong.

I toss and turn, trying not to think about Archion getting hurt—or worse. But eventually exhaustion takes over.

I fall into a fitful sleep waiting for Archion to come back to our bed.

## 23

## ARCHION

*T*he sky has that hint of dark gray that it gets just before dawn.

I walk through the city streets with the other Zmaj, our group slowly dwindling as we each return to our respective quarters.

Impatience beats at me as I enter our building. I have never had this great of a desire to return home. Or ever thought of a temporary place as home before. The thought gives me pause. I suppose home is now wherever Nora is.

I open the door to our shared apartment and step inside noiselessly. It is dark, quiet. The only sound is Nora's steady breathing as she sleeps.

Moving silently, I stop beside the bed, something inside me settling as I watch my love, safe and sound. I do not slide in next to her right away, wanting just to absorb the sight of her for a moment.

This female, my mate, has become near everything to me. There are no questions in me anymore when it comes to her.

I will take her home with me. The Order will accept her. The Elders will have no choice in the matter.

I appreciate Visidion's trust because it makes the trip easier, and I believe there may be opportunities for trade, an opportunity for an alliance of some kind. Though anything I can reveal to Visidion depends solely on the Order. How much they will allow me to expose in the face of real trade opportunities.

But I do not want to think of that now. For tonight, I want to simply enjoy the love of a millennia.

I slide under the covers at last, pull Nora into my arms, and kiss her soft mouth.

Her eyes flutter open.

"How did it go?" she murmurs, kissing me back, her arms rising to pull me in even closer.

The question is clear in her eyes when she pulls back. I answer it.

"There was no trouble," I reassure her. "Nobody was significantly hurt."

I do not add yet that we could tell that the invaders recognized me from my earlier decoy attempts. Their reaction told me that they remembered I had led them on a fruitless chase. When they recognized me, they turned wary, eventually breaking off the battle and doubling back—possibly to gather more reinforcements. Their reaction did not go unnoticed.

Visidion remained unworried at the response. If anything, I could see it made him think of the Order and the possibility of an alliance. It encouraged him to seriously consider a relationship with the brothers of a Zmaj who could strike such fear into our mutual enemies.

"Quite impressive," he'd muttered, watching them retreat. "Very impressive, actually." The look he gave me afterwards was assessing, almost calculating.

"No trouble?" Nora asks, frowning. "But then why were

179

you gone for so long? Are you saying there wasn't anybody there? That doesn't make any—"

I press a finger against her lips. "Shh. Let us not talk of this quite yet," I say softly, my mouth just touching her neck, as I slide a hand down her side to grip her lush backside. "I would like to think of only you now."

Her face softens as I roll on top of her, her gaze heating.

"Yes," she murmurs. "I'd like that too."

She was sleeping in only her undergarments, an impediment that is quickly gone, along with my own clothing.

This time, the lovemaking is sensual, a homecoming. Her body is a lush feast, one I take my time with. I suck at her pert nipples until she is writhing underneath me, then I settle between her legs, licking at her delicious, hot taste. I hold her rounded thighs down, enjoying the way her body tenses underneath my mouth, the way she calls out my name.

"Archion!"

I lick at her, suck at her, until she goes limp underneath me. I could spend hours kissing her there, in that delicate, private place—the feminine heart of her. But I also want to be inside her. I rise up so we are face to face, and I kiss her swollen mouth as I nudge my erection into her. I am so hard I feel close to bursting. As I feel more often than not when I am near Nora.

I watch her face as I move inside her, holding myself up so I do not crush her delicate frame. She has a hot, wet, tight grip around me. I cannot imagine anywhere I would rather be. I have never felt this much. Not emotionally, not physically.

I told her hips, finding just the right position so I hit that small pleasure spot at the very top of her cleft. She cries out, freezing underneath me when pleasure overtakes her again.

I do not close my eyes, wanting to see every moment. She is so beautiful, so perfect. When she falls back on the bed, breathing hard, she opens her eyes. I lean down to kiss her again.

"You are mine, Nora," I whisper against her lips.

It is a mating claim, and though she does not yet know the ways of my Order, I know what my eyes are communicating along with my heart.

She is mine. There is no other for me. There is no turning back.

Her eyes are full of love, full of a softness that is all for me. She reaches up, slides her fingers into my hair, and pulls me down, sealing my words with a kiss that confirms her agreement.

My treasure. I will forever keep her safe. She is my happiness.

# EPILOGUE

## KHAL

Flaring my wings to ride the air and lighten my weight on the sand, I crest the next rise and scour the desert around me.

Nothing.

Only more sun baked red sand.

Clenching my jaw, I continue on, my eyes searching with a growing desperation that I keep a tight reign on. It is a struggle to contain my concern in the face of my still fruitless search.

Where is Archion?

This is not at all like my brother. Not at all like the responsible mentor and leader. The emotions I am suppressing are pushing me to imagine the worst. To dwell upon a scenario I do not want to. But I refuse to do so, refuse to let the negative thoughts take hold.

It is not possible that my brother could have met a terrible fate.

It simply is not.

For decades, Archion has been at the very top of the warrior line on this side of Tajss. An inarguable, objective fact. He has a risen so high among the ranks that he reports directly to the Council and only to the Council.

Nobody else.

So the fact that Tashak finally decided to send me to look for him is...troublesome. The seers aren't known for their patience and Archion is already unforgivable late at this point.

If he returns without a limb or maimed in some other horrifying way, he will be loosely forgiven. But he will never be seen in the revered fashion that he has enjoyed for so long.

Harsh, yes. But it is a fact that cannot be escaped.

It is a bad enough end.

But if he has...

I shake my head, continuing my forward momentum, my eyes scanning the area around me while I think.

There is no scenario where he would betray the Order. After a lifetime spent protecting and upholding our values and objectives, I cannot see it coming to pass.

Archion is above reproach. I refuse to even entertain the notion. Clenching my jaw, I cut off my thoughts ruthlessly. I am not on any productive line. Better I simply focus on the mind numbing task of searching the desert.

The Tajss suns beat down upon me as I cover the sand as quickly as possible, the scorching light a familiar burn against the skin left exposed by my robes.

I continue on the grid search I planned before I left, the painstaking method chosen so I do not miss anything by accident. Yes, it takes more time. But it is better to be thorough the first time rather than having to retrace my footsteps.

Not that it has mattered much thus far. As carefully as I look, I do not see tracks or any sign that the Order marked rifts have been used. No sign that anything larger than a small animal has been anywhere near here.

I ignore the pit that attempts to settle in my stomach, squashing it before it can grow to something larger and heavier. Archion is still here. My brother will return. There is no other option.

I frown feeling an odd sensation in my midsection directly after I mentally proclaim this. Like a tugging in my gut.

An answer?

I turn in the direction of the gentle but insistent pull, the feeling so distinct I know I am on the correct course.

"He is alive."

I whisper the words out loud, willing them to be so. Needing them to be so. I follow that feeling, holding onto it as tightly as I can. It is the only hope that I have seen for days upon days.

I need it. Need the fuel it provides. I stay out for most of the rest of the day, a renewed sense of purpose combining with a surge of energy, the two aiding me in traveling fast, keeping my eyes sharp.

But it does not matter. I still do not encounter anyone. Until, with a sinking stomach, I know it is too late to stay out much longer. Without the bright suns out during the day to guide me, I may very well miss tracks or other signs even if I come upon them. That would only set me back in my search, lead me astray.

So I force myself to turn back even though I want to keep searching, keep looking until my body gives way. But I know I cannot make decisions based on emotions alone.

That will not serve Archion well. Or anyone for that matter.

So I settle a neutral look upon my face, a trained expression of duty designed to hide my emotions, and report my findings to Tashak. It does not take long. After all, I have found nothing.

But Tashak's reaction shocks me.

Raising his hand, he rests it upon my shoulder in a consoling fashion. His jewel toned robes rustle with the movement, his staff still held firmly in his other hand.

I look down at that strong hand, breathing in deeply. I swallow passed the lump in my throat, refusing to entertain the thought that I am certain the seer is building up towards.

"I know he is still alive," I say, preempting what I know he planned to voice. I cannot allow him to say the words. I place my hand over my midsection. "I feel it here."

I try to convey the feeling, the surety, in an effort to convince him. But when the seer nods, I can see that he may just to be humoring me.

"Only time will tell us what has happened to Archion," he replies after a brief pause. "We will wait. And see."

The words are neutral. But the tone is not.

A slight frown touches his face, a hint of danger or perhaps trepidation lacing the statement and his expression. It is clear that he would rather the former be true than the latter.

But the latter is not possible. My brother is alive. I feel it inside myself, a knowing that will not be denied.

And I refuse to believe otherwise.

No matter what any seer tells me.

*THE END*

# ABOUT THE AUTHOR

USA Today Bestselling Author of fantasy and scifi romance, Miranda Martin's books feature larger than life heroes with out-of-this-world anatomy and smart heroines destined to save the world. As a little girl she would sneak off with her nose in a book, dreaming of magical realms. Today she brings those fantasies to life and adores every fan who chooses to live in them for a while.

She was born and raised in southern Virginia, but as a veteran she's traveled to places like Korea, Hawaii and good 'ole Texas. Now she's settled in Kansas, the heart of America, with her husband and daughters. Her favorite animals are dragons, unicorns and cats. If she's not writing, you can still find her tucked away somewhere with a warm blanket and her nose in a book.

*Get in touch!*
mirandamartinromance.com
miranda@mirandamartinromance.com

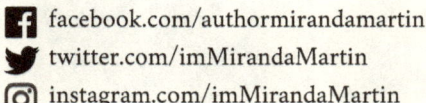

facebook.com/authormirandamartin
twitter.com/imMirandaMartin
instagram.com/imMirandaMartin